HARLEQUIN

25% OFF LIST PRICE $5.25 **$3.93** YOU PAY

Desire

THE PREGNANCY AFFAIR

ELIZABETH BEVARLY

NEW YORK TIMES
BESTSELLING AUTHOR

"It's not a good idea," she said quietly.

He circled her wrists with deft fingers and moved both their hands behind her back, then leaned in again. "Oh, I think it's a very good idea."

He started to lower his mouth to hers, and, God help her, Renny stood still for the merest of seconds and waited for him to make contact. He was just so unbelievably... So extremely... So totally, totally...

His lips brushed hers lightly...once, twice, three times, four. Heat splashed in her belly, spilling through her torso and into her limbs, warming parts of her she hadn't even realized were cold. Then he stepped closer and covered her mouth completely with his, and those parts fairly burst into flames. For another scandalous, too-brief moment, she reveled in the fantasy that was Tate Hawthorne and the wild ride it promised. Then, nimbly, she tugged her hands free of his and somehow broke away to scurry to the kitchenette.

"Hey, are you as hungry as I am?" she asked when she got there.

Belatedly, she realized the glaring double entendre of the question.

* * *

The Pregnancy Affair is part of the Accidental Heirs series: First they find their fortunes, then they find love.

Dear Reader,

If you've read my older books, you know I have a not-so-secret fascination with the mob. I have no idea why. Maybe it's because of the stories my grandmother told me about her mobster neighbors in the Chicago apartment house where she lived in the 1930s. Maybe it's because of nicknames like "Baby Fat Larry," "Vinny Carwash" and "Willie Potatoes." Maybe it's the hats.

Anyway, I shouldn't have been surprised when the mob popped up in a book again. What did surprise me was realizing my hero was a made man. Okay, a made toddler. Fortunately, Tate Hawthorne escaped into the witness protection program with his parents at the age of three. Just as well, really. "Tate the Venture Capitalist" doesn't have the right ring.

*Un*fortunately, his government-assigned identity has been blown, so he's taken into protective custody again. Worse, he's trapped there with Renny Twigg, the woman who accidentally outed him, threw his entire existence into turmoil and potentially endangered his life. Worst of all, the feds have hidden them in the wilds of Wisconsin without so much as basic cable or dial-up internet. Or a post-1999 issue of *Maxim*. Or a decent wine list. Or, you know, clothes.

It's going to be a long five days. Whatever will Tate and Renny do to pass the time? Especially when the Scrabble game is missing most of its vowels? And what happens when Renny gets home and discovers she's brought a fairly life-changing souvenir with her? It's going to be a long nine months...

Happy reading!

Elizabeth

ELIZABETH BEVARLY

THE PREGNANCY AFFAIR

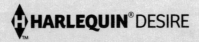

Recycling programs
for this product may
not exist in your area.

ISBN-13: 978-0-373-83828-8

The Pregnancy Affair

Copyright © 2017 by Elizabeth Bevarly

Printed in U.S.A.

Elizabeth Bevarly is an award-winning, *New York Times* bestselling author of more than seventy books. Although she has made her home in exotic places like San Juan, Puerto Rico, and Haddonfield, New Jersey, she's now happily settled back in her native Kentucky. When she's not writing, she's binge watching British TV shows on Netflix or making soup out of whatever she finds in the freezer. Visit her at www.elizabethbevarly.com.

Books by Elizabeth Bevarly

Harlequin Desire

Taming the Prince
Taming the Beastly M.D.
Married to His Business
The Billionaire Gets His Way
My Fair Billionaire
Caught in the Billionaire's Embrace

The Accidental Heirs

Only on His Terms
A CEO in Her Stocking
The Pregnancy Affair

Visit her Author Profile page at Harlequin.com, or elizabethbevarly.com, for more titles!

For my grandmother,
Ruth Elizabeth Hensley Bevarly,
who told me some really great stories
when I was a kid.

I miss you, Nanno.

One

Renny Twigg threw her car into Park and gazed at the Tudor-style house beyond her windshield. Or maybe she should say Tudor-style *castle* beyond her windshield. Its walls were made of majestically arranged stones and climbed a full three stories, and they were tatted here and there with just the right amount of ivy. Its stained glass mullion windows sparkled in the late-morning sunlight as if they'd been fashioned from gemstones, and its turrets—one on each side—stretched even higher than the slate roof, looking as if they'd been carved by the hand of a Renaissance artist. The lot on which the mansion sat was nearly a city-state unto itself, green and glorious and landscaped with more flowering shrubs than a Spring Hill catalog.

There was rich, and then there was *rich*. The first was something with which Renny had a more-than-nodding acquaintance. She'd come from a long line of powerful attorneys, financiers and carpetbaggers, the first of whom had arrived in this country hundreds of years ago to capitalize on the hugely exploitable land and its even more exploitable colonists. The Twiggs who followed had adopted the tradition and run with it, fattening the family coffers more with each ensuing generation. She'd grown up in a big white Cape Cod in Greenwich, Connecticut, had donned tidy blue uniforms for tony private schools before heading off to be a Harvard legacy, and had worn a sparkly tiara—with real diamonds—for her debut eleven years ago. Renny Twigg knew what it was to be rich.

She eyed the massive structure and its imperious gardens again. Tate Hawthorne was obviously *rich*.

She inhaled a fortifying breath and tucked an unruly dark brown tendril back into the otherwise flawless chignon at her nape. Then she checked her lipstick in the rearview mirror, breathed into her hand to ensure that there were no lingering traces of her breakfast burrito and smoothed a hand over her tan linen suit. Yep. She was perfectly acceptable for her meeting with the man her employer had assigned her to locate. *So go ahead, Renny. What are you waiting for?*

She eyed the massive mansion again. What she was waiting for was to see if a dragon would come swooping down from one of those turrets to carry her off for his own breakfast. In spite of the colorful landscaping and bright blue summer sky that framed it, the place just had that look about it. As if its owner were some brooding, overbearing Rochester who might very well lock her away in his attic.

Oh, stop it, she told herself. Tate Hawthorne was one of Chicago's savviest investors by day and one of its most notorious playboys by night. From what she'd learned of him, the only thing he dedicated more time to than making money was spending it. Mostly on fast, lustrous cars and fast, leggy redheads. Renny was five foot three in her kitten heels and had driven up in a rented Buick. She was the last kind of woman a man like him would want to stash away for nefarious purposes.

Even if his origins were pretty freakin' nefarious.

She opened the car door and stepped out onto the cobbled drive. Although it was only June, the heat was oppressive. She hurried to the front door, rehearsing in her head one last time the most tactful way to relay all the news she had for Tate Hawthorne.

Like how he wasn't really Tate Hawthorne.

Renny's employer, Tarrant, Fiver & Twigg—though the Twigg in the name was her father, not her—was a law firm that went by many descriptions. Probate researchers. Estate detectives. Heir hunters. Their services were enlisted by the state of New York when someone died without a will and no next of kin was known or when the next of kin was known but his or her whereabouts were not.

That second option had brought her to Highland Park, a suburb of Chicago for people who were *rich*. Bennett Tarrant, president and senior probate researcher, had given the job to Renny because she always found the heir she was looking for. Well, except for that one time. And also because she was the only probate researcher available at the time who didn't have anything on her plate that couldn't be scraped off with a quick fork to the archives room. For lack of a better analogy. That breakfast burrito had, after all, been hours ago.

And although he hadn't said so specifically, she was pretty sure another reason Bennett had assigned her the job was to offer her a chance to redeem herself for that one time she hadn't been able to find the heir she was looking for. Locating someone who would be extremely hard to locate—like Tate Hawthorne—and doing so without screwing it up would make Renny a shoo-in for the promotion that had been eluding her, something that would make her father very proud.

Not to mention make him stop looking at her as if she were a complete screwup.

In the meantime, Renny was proud of herself. It took skill and talent to find someone who had been buried in the federal Witness Protection Program along with the rest of his immediate family nearly three decades ago. Well, it took those things and also a friend from high school who had mad hacking skills and could find anything—or anyone—on the internet. But that was beside the point. The point was Renny had found the heir she was looking for, thanks to said friend. Which would, she hoped, put her back on the fast track at Tarrant, Fiver & Twigg and get her father off her back for that one tiny blip that had changed the company's 100% find rate to a 99.9999% find rate, and jeez, Dad, it wasn't like she'd lost that one on purpose, so just give her a break. *Man.*

She rang the doorbell and fanned herself with her portfolio as she waited for a response, since, judging by the size of the house, it could be days before anyone made their way to the front door. So she was surprised to be caught midfan when the door opened almost immediately. Thankfully, it wasn't Tate Hawthorne who answered. It was a liveried butler, who looked to be about the same age as one of the founding fathers. If the founding fathers were still alive, she meant.

"Good morning," Thomas Jefferson greeted her. "Miss Twigg, I presume?"

She nodded. She had contacted Tate Hawthorne earlier this week—or, rather, she had contacted his assistant Aurora, who, Renny hadn't been able to help thinking, sounded like a fast, leggy redhead— and set up a meeting with him for the only fifteen minutes the guy seemed to have available for the entire month of June. And that was only because, Aurora had told her, he could cut short by a teensy bit his preparation for his regular Saturday polo match.

"Hello," Renny replied. "I'm sorry to be a bit early. I was hoping Mr. Hawthorne might be able to squeeze in another ten or fifteen minutes for our meeting. What I have to tell him is kind of—" *life changing* was the phrase that came to mind, but it sounded a little melodramatic "—important. What I have to tell Mr. Hawthorne is kind of important." And also life changing.

"All of Mr. Hawthorne's meetings are important," Thomas Jefferson said indulgently.

Of course they were. Hence his having only fifteen minutes in the entire month of June for Renny. "Nevertheless," she began.

"It's all right, Madison," a booming baritone interrupted her.

Renny gazed past the butler at a man who had appeared behind him and who had to be Tate Hawthorne. She knew that, because he looked really, really *rich*.

His sable hair was cropped short, his skin was sun burnished to the color of a gold doubloon and his gray eyes shone like platinum. He was dressed in a polo uniform—equestrian, not water, unfortunately, because a body like his would have seriously rocked a Speedo—in hues of more precious materials, from the coppery shirt to the chocolate-truffle jodhpurs, to the front-zipper mahogany boots that climbed up over his knees with their protective padding. All of it skintight over taut thighs, a sinewy torso, salient biceps and shoulders broader than the Brooklyn Bridge. It was all Renny could do to not drool.

Unfortunately, she wasn't as lucky in keeping herself from greeting him less than professionally. "Hiya." Immediately, she realized her loss of composure and pheromones and amended, "I mean… hello, Mr. Hawthorne."

"Hello yourself, Ms…." He halted. "I'm sorry. Aurora included your name with the appointment, but I've been working on something else this morning, and it's slipped my mind. And, well…you are a bit early."

He seemed genuinely contrite that he was at a loss for her name, something for which Renny had to give him credit. Not just because he was being so polite about her having impinged on his time after being told he didn't have much to spare, but because, in her experience, most high-powered business types didn't feel contrite about anything, least of all forgetting the name of a junior associate from a law firm they never had dealings with.

Madison the butler moved aside, and she murmured her thanks as she stepped past him into the foyer. She withdrew a business card from inside her jacket and extended it toward Tate Hawthorne.

"I'm Renata Twigg," she said. Not that she'd felt like a *Renata* a single day in her life, because Renata sounded like, well, a tall, leggy redhead. Renny had no idea what her mother had been thinking to want to name her that, or what her father had been thinking to insist it be the name she used professionally. "I represent Tarrant, Fiver & Twigg, attorneys," she concluded.

He took the card from her but didn't look at it. Instead, he looked at Renny. With way too much interest for her sanity and saliva glands. And—okay, okay—her pheromones, too.

"Renata," he said, fairly purring the word in a way that reminded her of velvet and cognac. And suddenly, for some reason, Renny didn't mind her given name at all.

"Thank you so much for making time to meet with me this morning," she said. "I know you must be very busy." Duh.

She drove her gaze around the massive black-and-white-tiled foyer to the half-dozen ways out of it—two doors to her right, two doors to her left, and one more framed by a curving staircase that led to the second floor.

"Um, is there someplace we can talk?" she asked.

For a moment, Tate Hawthorne said nothing, only continued to gaze at her in that mind-scrambling, gland-addling way. Finally, he said, "Of course."

He extended a hand to his left to indicate Renny should precede him. Which she would have done, had she had a clue where he wanted her to go. He could have been gesturing at the doors to her left, the staircase, or to the exit behind himself. He seemed to realize the ambiguity of his action, too, and threw her an apologetic smile that just made him even more charming. As if he needed that. As if *she* needed that.

"My office is this way," he told her.

He opted for the exit behind himself, and Renny followed. They passed another eight or nine—hundred—rooms before he finally turned into one that looked more like a library than an office, so stuffed to the ceiling was it with books. There was a desk tucked into a corner, facing to look out the window at a green space behind the house that was even more idyllic than the scene in front, and topped with a state-of-the-art computer and tidy piles of paperwork. Also sitting there was a polo helmet that matched his uniform, so she gathered he was in here when she arrived, trying to cram in more work before heading out to play. The guy clearly took both his business and his pleasure seriously.

"Please, have a seat," he said, gesturing toward a leather-bound chair that had probably cost more than the gross national product of some sovereign nations. Then he spun around his desk chair—also leather, but smaller—and folded himself into it.

Renny tried not to notice how his clothing seemed to cling even more tightly when he was seated, and she tried not to think about how much she suddenly wanted to drop to her knees in front of him to unzip his boots. With her teeth. Instead, she opened her portfolio and withdrew the handful of documents she'd brought with her to support what was sure to sound like a made-for-cable movie on one of the channels that was *way* high up the dial.

"Mr. Hawthorne," she began.

"Tate," he corrected her.

She looked up from her task, her gaze fastening with his again. Those eyes. So pale and gray and cool for a man who seemed so deep and dark and hot. "Excuse me?" she said without thinking.

He smiled again. She tried not to spontaneously combust. "Call me Tate," he said. "'Mr. Hawthorne' is what they call me at work."

This wasn't work? she wanted to ask. It was work to her. At least, it had been before he smiled in a way that made clear his thoughts were closer to plea-sure at the moment than they were to business. And, thanks to that smile, now Renny's were, too.

"Ah," she started again. Probably best not to call him anything at all. Especially since the only thing coming to mind at the moment was... Um, never mind. "Are you familiar with the name Joseph Bacco?" she asked.

A spark of something flickered in his eyes, then disappeared. "Maybe?" he said. "Something in the news a while back? I don't remember the context, though."

Renny wasn't sure how far Joseph Bacco's influ-ence might have traveled beyond New York and New Jersey, but he'd been a colorful-enough character in his time to warrant the occasional story in maga-zines or true-crime shows on TV. And his death had indeed made national news. She tried another tack.

"How about the name 'Joey the Knife?'"

Tate's smile this time was tinted more with humor than with heat. And, gee, why was it suddenly so easy for her to think of him as *Tate*?

"No," he replied.

"'Bulletproof Bacco'?" she asked, trying another of Joseph Bacco's distinctive monikers.

"Ms. Twigg—"

"Renny," she said before she could stop herself. And immediately regretted not being able to stop herself. What was she thinking? She never invited clients to use her first name. And only Bennett Tarrant and her father called her Renny at work, because they'd both known her since the day she was born.

Tate's gaze turned hot again. "I thought you said your name is Renata."

She swallowed hard. "It is. But everyone calls me Renny."

At least everyone who wasn't tied to her by business. Which Tate most certainly was. So why had she extended the invitation to him? And why did she want to extend more invitations to him? None of which included him calling her by name and all of which had him calling her hot, earthy things as he buried himself inside her and drove her to the brink of—

"You don't seem like a Renny," he said. Just in the nick of time, too. The last thing she needed was to have an impromptu orgasm in front of a client. Talk about a black mark on her permanent record.

"I don't?" she asked, in a voice normally used only when having an impromptu orgasm. Maybe he wouldn't notice.

Judging by the way his pupils dilated, though, she was pretty sure he did. Even so, his own voice was level—if a tad warm—when he said, "No. You seem like a Renata to me."

Well, this was news to Renny. No one thought she was a Renata. Even her own parents had given up calling her that the day she stripped off her pink tutu in ballet class and decreed she would instead play football, like her brothers. Ultimately, she and her parents had compromised on archery, but still. *Renata* had gone the way of the pink tutu decades ago.

"Uh…" she said eloquently. Damn. What had they been talking about?

"Bulletproof Bacco," he repeated.

Right. Joey the Knife. Nothing like references to ammunition and cutlery to put a damper on thoughts of… Um, never mind.

"That doesn't sound like the name of someone I'd run into at the Chicago Merc," he continued.

She tried one last time. "How about the 'Iron Don'?" she asked. "Does that name ring a bell?"

The light came back into his eyes, and this time it stayed lit. "Right," he said. "The mobster."

"*Alleged* mobster," Renny corrected him. Since no one had ever been able to pin any charges on Joey the Knife that hadn't slid right off him like butter from a hot, well, knife. Though she was reasonably sure that wasn't why he'd earned that particular nickname.

"From New York, I think," Tate said. "His death was in the news a couple of months ago. Everyone kept commenting that he'd lived to be the oldest organized-crime figure ever and died of old age instead of…something else."

"*Alleged* organized-crime figure," Renny corrected him again. "And, yes, he's the man I'm talking about."

Tate glanced at his watch, then back at Renny. All heated glances and flirtation aside, the man was obviously on a schedule he intended to keep. "And he has bearing on this meeting…how?"

Renny handed him the first of the records she'd brought with her—a copy of his original birth certificate from New Jersey, much different from the one he had now from Indiana, which he'd been using since the fifth grade. The name printed on it, however, wasn't Tate Hawthorne, as he had come to be known after his stepfather adopted him. Nor was it Tate Carson, as he had been known before that. The name on this record was—

"Joseph Anthony Bacco the Third?" he asked.

"Grandson of Joseph Anthony Bacco Senior," Renny said. "Aka Joey the Knife. Aka Bulletproof Bacco. Aka the Iron Don."

"And why are you showing me a birth certificate that belongs to a mobster's grandson?"

Renny started to correct him, but he hastily amended, "*Alleged* mobster's grandson. What does Joseph the Third, or Joseph Senior, for that matter, have to do with me?"

She withdrew from her portfolio a photograph, one of several she had from the 1980s. In it, a man in his sixties was seated on a sofa beside a man in his twenties who was holding a toddler in his lap. She handed it to Tate, who accepted it warily. For a moment, he gazed at her through narrowed eyes, and somehow she sensed there was a part of him that knew what was coming. But he only dropped his gaze to the photo.

"The picture is from Joseph Bacco's estate," Renny said. "The older man is Joseph Anthony Bacco Senior, and the younger man beside him is—"

"My father," Tate finished for her. "I don't remember him very well. He died when I was four. But I have some photographs of him and recognize him from those. I assume the little boy he's holding is me."

"Yes."

"Meaning my father was an acquaintance of the Iron Don," he gathered, still looking at the photograph.

"He was more than an acquaintance," she told him. "Your father was Joseph Anthony Bacco Junior."

At this, Tate snapped his head back up to look at her. "That's impossible. My father's name was James Carson. He worked in a hardware store in Terre Haute, Indiana. It burned down when I was four. He was killed in the fire."

Renny sifted through her documents until she located two more she was looking for. "James Carson was the name your father was given by the federal marshals before they placed him and your mother and you in the Witness Protection Program when you were two years old. Your family entered WITSEC after your father was the star witness at a murder trial against one of Joseph Bacco's capos, Carmine Tomasi. Your father also gave testimony against a half-dozen others in the organization that led to a host of arrests and convictions for racketeering crimes."

She glanced down at the record on top. "Your mother became Natalie Carson, and you became Tate Carson. You all received new Social Security numbers and birth dates. The feds moved the three of you from Passaic, New Jersey, to Terre Haute, and both your parents were given new jobs. Your father at the hardware store and your mother at a local insurance company."

Renny handed him copies of documents to support those assertions, too. She'd received everything she had to support her story via snail mail at her condo a few days ago, from her high school friend with the mad hacking skills. They were records she was reasonably certain she wasn't supposed to have—she'd known better than to ask where they came from. The only reason Phoebe had helped her out in the first place was because Renny (A) promised to never divulge her source and (B) pulled in a favor she'd been owed by Phoebe since a sleepover thirteen years ago, a favor that might or might not have something to do with a certain boy in home-room named Kyle.

These records, too, Tate accepted from her, but this time, his gaze fell to them immediately, and he voraciously read every word. When he looked up again, his pale gray eyes were stormy. "Are you try-ing to tell me…?"

She decided it would probably be best to just spill the news as cleanly and quickly as possible and fol-low up with details in the inevitable Q&A.

"You're Joey the Knife's grandson and legal heir. In spite of your father's having ratted out some of his associates, your grandfather left his entire estate to you, as you're the oldest son of his oldest son, and that's what hundreds of years of Bacco tradition dic-tates. What's more, it was Joey's dying wish that you assume his position as head of the family and take over all of his businesses after his death.

"In short, Mr. Hawthorne," Renny concluded, "Jo-seph Anthony Bacco Senior has crowned you the new Iron Don."

Two

It took a minute for Tate to process everything Renata Twigg had dropped into his lap. And even then, he wasn't sure he was processing it correctly. It was just too far outside his scope of experience. Too hard to believe. Too weird.

Renata seemed to sense his state of confusion, because she said, "Mr. Hawthorne? Do you have any questions?"

Oh, sure. He had questions. A couple. Million. Now if he could just get one of them to settle in his brain long enough for him to put voice to it...

One that finally settled enough to come out was

"How could a mobster want to leave his fortune to the son of a man who double-crossed him?"

"*Alleged* mobster," Renata corrected him. Again. Not that Tate for a moment believed there could be any shades of gray about a guy named Joey the Knife.

"If I really am Joseph Bacco's grandson," he began.

"You are definitely Joseph Bacco's grandson."

"Then why would he want to have anything to do with me? My father—his son—turned him in to the feds. Wouldn't that kind of negate any familial obligation that existed prior to that? Or... I don't know... put a contract on my father's head?"

"Actually, your father didn't turn Joey in to the feds," Renata said. "Or any other member of the immediate Bacco family. All the information he gave to the feds had to do with other members of the organization. And he only gave up that information because the feds had enough evidence of his own criminal activity to put him away for forty years."

"*My* father?" Tate said incredulously. "Committed crimes worthy of forty years in prison?"

Renata nodded. "I'm afraid so. Nothing violent," she hastened to reassure him. "The charges against your father were for fraud, bribery, embezzlement and money laundering. Lots and lots of fraud, bribery, embezzlement and money laundering. There was never any evidence that he was involved in anything more than that. He was highly placed in your grand-father's business. Wise guys that high up... Uh... I mean...*guys* that high up don't get their hands that dirty. But your father didn't want to go to prison for forty years." She smiled halfheartedly. "He wanted to watch his little son grow up."

Tate tried to take some comfort in that. Even so, it was hard to imagine James Carson involved in cor-ruption. His memories of his father were hazy, but they evoked only feelings of affection and warmth. His dad, from what he recalled, was a good guy.

"Anyway," Renata continued, "because your father never fingered anyone in the Bacco family proper—in fact, his agreement with the feds stated he would absolutely not, under any condition, in-criminate his family—Joey the Knife never sought a vendetta. He really loved his son," she added. "I think a part of him kind of understood why your fa-ther did what he did, so he could be with his son. But even more important, I think Joey really loved you—his first grandson. And since you had nothing to do with what your father did, he wanted you to come back and take your rightful place in the family."

As what? Tate wondered. What kind of nickname would suit the lifestyle he'd assumed instead? Bot-tom Line Bacco? Joey the Venture Capitalist? Some-how those just didn't have the same ring. Or did they? Renata had just said his grandfather had businesses. Maybe there was a bit of Bacco in Tate yet.

"You said my grandfather had businesses?" he asked.

She withdrew another collection of papers from her portfolio. "Several. He wants to put you in charge of Cosa Nostra, for one thing."

"Yeah, you just pretty much said that when you told me he wants me to be the new Iron Don."

She shook her head. "No, not that Cosa Nostra. That *alleged* one, I mean. Cosa Nostra is the name of a chain of Italian restaurants he owned up and down the Jersey shore."

Tate took this page from her, too, and quickly scanned the figures. Unless Cosa Nostra was a three-star Michelin restaurant that served minestrone for five hundred bucks a bowl, its profits were way too high to be on the up-and-up.

"Yeah, these places look completely legitimate," he said wryly.

"By all accounts, they are. Joey bought them with the proceeds from his waste-management business and his construction company."

Yep. Totally legit.

"Since your grandfather's death in the spring, everything's been run by his second in command, who—" she hesitated for a moment "—who's married to your father's sister."

Tate remembered then that Renata had mentioned there were other members of the "immediate" Bacco family. He'd been an only child all his life and had been under the impression that both of his parents were, too. At least, that was what his mother had always told him to explain why he didn't have any aunts or uncles or cousins, the way all his classmates did.

Of course, all these new revelations might also explain why she'd always seemed to go out of her way to ensure that he stayed an only child—not just in the birth sense but in the social sense, too. She'd never encouraged him to make friends when he was growing up and had, in fact, been wary of anyone who tried to get too close. Although he'd had a handful of friends at school, she'd never let him invite any of them home or allowed him to play at their houses. He'd never had birthday parties or sleepovers, hadn't been able to join Cub Scouts or play team sports or attend summer camp.

His childhood hadn't exactly been happy, thanks to his solitary state. He'd always thought his mother was just overprotective. Now he wondered if she'd spent the rest of her life watching their backs. He wished he could ask her about all this, but he'd lost her to cancer when he was in college. His stepfather—who might or might not have known about anything—had been quite a bit older than his mother and had died less than a year later. There was no one around who could verify any of this for Tate. No one except Renata Twigg.

"I have other family members?" he asked.

She nodded. "Your father had two sisters, both older than him. Denise is married to Joseph Bacco's second in command, Nicholas DiNapoli, aka Nicky the Pistol."

"My aunt is mobbed up, too?"

"Allegedly. His other sister, Lucia, is married to Handsome Mickey Testa, the manager of one of Joey's casinos."

Did anyone in the mob *not* have a nickname? "Do I have cousins by them?" Tate asked.

She flipped another page. "Yes. Denise and Nicky have Sal the Stiletto, Dirty Dominic and... Oh. This is different."

"What?"

"Angie the Flamethrower. Gotta give a girl credit for that. And Lucia and Mickey have Concetta."

"Who I assume is Connie the something."

"Well, right now she's Connie the economics major at Cornell. But I wouldn't rule anything out."

"So my entire family are mobsters."

"Alleged mobsters. And an economics major."

Renata gazed at him with what could have been compassion or condemnation. He had no idea. She was very good at hiding whatever she was thinking. Well, except for a couple of times when he was pretty sure she'd been thinking some of the same things he'd been thinking, most of them X-rated. Her espresso eyes were enormous and thickly lashed, her dark hair was pulled back into the most severe hairstyle he'd ever seen and her buff-colored suit was conservative in the extreme.

Even so, he couldn't shake the feeling that the image she presented to the world had nothing to do with the person she really was. Although she looked professional, capable and no-nonsense, there was something about her that suggested she wanted to be none of those things.

"So this law firm you work for," Tate said. "Does it handle a lot of, ah, *alleged* mob work?"

She shook her head. "Tarrant, Fiver & Twigg is about as white-shoe a firm as you're going to find. But, according to my father—who's the current Twigg in the name—Joey the Knife and Bennett Tarrant's father had some kind of shared history when they were young. No one's ever asked what. But it was Bennett's father who took him on as a client back in the sixties, and Bennett honored his father's wish that he always look after Joey."

"So Joey must have had some redeeming values then."

"He loved his son. And he loved his grandson. I'd say that makes up for a lot."

Tate looked down at the sheet that had his mother's original information on it. She had been Isabel Danson before she married Joseph Jr.

When Renata saw where his attention had fallen, she told him, "For what it's worth, your mother's family wasn't connected. Allegedly or otherwise."

"Do I have family on that side, too?"

"I'm sorry, no. She was an only child."

At least something his mother had told him was true.

"Her parents, both deceased now, were florists."

Finally. Something beautiful to counter all the luridness of his heritage.

"So what do my aunts, uncles and cousins think of this?" Tate asked, looking up again. "Seems to me they might all be a little put off by Joey's wanting a total stranger to come in and take over. Especially when that stranger's father ratted out other members of the organization."

"Right now, I'm the only person who knows you're Joseph Anthony Bacco the Third," Renata assured him. "Because of the delicate nature of the situation, I haven't even told the senior partners of Tarrant, Fiver & Twigg who or where you are. Only that I found you and would contact you about Joey's final wishes. I haven't told the Baccos even that much."

"And if I decide I'd just as soon not accept my grandfather's legacy?" Tate asked.

Since it went without saying he wouldn't be accepting his grandfather's legacy. He wasn't sure yet how he felt about accepting his grandfather's family, though. The blood one, not the professional one. A lot of that depended on whether or not they were accepting of him. For all he knew, they were already dialing 1-800-Vendetta.

"The surviving Baccos were all aware of Joey's wishes," Renata said. "They've known all along that he wanted his missing grandson to be found and take over after his death. He never made any secret of that. But I don't know how they felt about that or if they even expected anyone to ever be able to find you. If you don't accept your grandfather's legacy, then Joey wants everything to go to Denise and her husband so they can continue the tradition with their oldest son. That may be what they've been assuming would happen all along."

"I don't want to accept my grandfather's legacy," Tate said plainly.

"Then I'll relay your wishes to the rest of the family," Renata told him. "And unless you decide to approach them yourself, they'll never know who or where you are. No one will. I'll take the secret of your identity to my grave."

Tate nodded. Somehow, he trusted Renata Twigg to do exactly that. But he still wasn't sure what he wanted to do about his identity. As a child, he'd often fantasized about having a family. Just not one that was quite so *famiglia*. He'd be lying, though, if he said there wasn't a part of him that was wondering what it would be like to be a Bacco.

"It's my aunt's and cousins' birthright as much as it is mine," Tate said. "They were a part of my grandfather's life and lifestyle. And I—"

He halted there, still a little thrown by everything he'd learned. He searched his brain for something that might negate everything Renata had told him. But his memories of his father were hazy. The only clear ones were of the day he died. Tate remembered the police coming to their house, his mother crying and a guy in a suit trying to console her. As an adult looking back, he'd always figured the guy was from the insurance company, there to handle his father's life-insurance policy or something. But after what Renata had told him, the guy might have been a fed, there to ensure that his mother was still protected.

He conjured more memories, out of sequence and context. His father swinging him in the ocean surf when he was very little. The two of them visiting an ancient-looking monkey house of some zoo. His father dancing him around in the kitchen, singing "Eh, Cumpari!," a song Tate had never heard anywhere else except for when…

Oh, God. Except for when Talia Shire sang it in *The Godfather, Part III.*

"There are more photos," he heard Renata say from what seemed a very great distance. "Joey had several framed ones of you and him on shelves in his office until the day he died."

Tate looked at the photo in his hand again. The Iron Don honestly looked like he could be anyone's grandfather—white hair and mustache, short-sleeved shirt and trousers, grinning at the boy in the picture as if he were his most cherished companion. There were no gold chains, no jogging suits, nothing to fit the stereotype at all. Just an old man happy to be with his family. Yet Tate couldn't remember him.

On some level, though, a lot of what Renata said explained his memories. He couldn't recall taking a long road trip anywhere until his mother married William Hawthorne. So how could he have been in the ocean when he was so young? Unless he'd lived in a state that had a coastline. Like New Jersey. And there were no ancient-looking monkey houses in this part of the country. But some zoos in the Northeast had lots of old buildings like that.

He looked at Renata Twigg. "I'm the grandson of a mobster," he said softly. This time, the remark was a statement, not a question.

"Alleged mobster," she qualified again, just as quietly.

"But real grandson."

"Yes."

So Tate really did have family out there with whom he would have grown up had things been different. He would have attended birthday parties and weddings and graduations for them. Vacationed with them. Played with them. He wouldn't have spent his childhood alone. Strangely, if his father had gone into the family's very abnormal business, Tate might have had a very normal childhood.

The pounding of footsteps suddenly erupted in the hall outside his office. Tate looked up just in time to see a man in a suit, followed by a harried Madison, come hurrying through the door. When he halted, the man's jacket swung open enough to reveal a shoulder holster with a weapon tucked inside. Tate was reaching for his phone to hit 9-1-1 when his presumed assailant flipped open a leather case in his hand to reveal a badge with a silver star.

"Inspector Terrence Grady," the man said. He reminded Tate of someone. An older version of Laurence Fishburne, maybe. "United States Marshals Service. Tate Hawthorne, you'll have to come with me immediately."

"Sir, he pushed right past me," Madison said. "I tried to—"

"It's all right, Madison," Tate said as he stood.

Renata stood at the same time, though she didn't cut quite as imposing a figure as Tate was trying to achieve himself. Actually, it was kind of hard to tell if she'd stood at all, because she barely came to his shoulder. Small women. He never knew what to do with small women. They were just so…small. But Renata Twigg had already inspired a few interesting ideas in his head. Given the chance—which, for some reason, he was hoping for—he was sure he could find a few more.

Instead of responding to Inspector Grady, Tate, for some reason, looked at Renata. He expected her to look as confused as he felt over the marshal's sudden appearance. Instead, a blush was blooming on her cheeks, and she was steadfastly avoiding his gaze.

He turned back to the marshal. "I don't understand. Why should I go anywhere with you?"

Grady—maybe not Laurence Fishburne, but he looked like *someone* Tate knew—said, "I can explain on the way."

"On the way where?"

"We need to get you someplace safe, Mr. Hawthorne." And then, just in case Tate had missed that part before, he added, more emphatically this time, *"Immediately."*

Tate straightened to his full six-three and leveled his most menacing gaze on the marshal. "I'm not going anywhere. What the hell does a federal marshal have to do with—"

Hang on. Didn't federal marshals run the Witness

Protection Program? Tate looked at Renata again. She was looking at something on the other side of the room and fiddling with the top button of her shirt in a way that might have been kind of interesting in a different situation. Under the circumstances…

"Renata," he said softly.

She was still looking at the wall and twisting her button, but she lifted her other hand to the twist of dark hair at her nape, giving it a few little pats, even though not a single hair was out of place. "Yes?"

"Do you have any idea why a federal marshal would show up at my front door less than an hour after you did?"

"Mr. Hawthorne," Grady interrupted.

Tate held up a hand to halt him. "Renata?" he repeated.

Finally, she turned her head to look at him. This time he knew exactly what she was thinking. Her eyes were a veritable window to her soul. And what Renata's soul was saying just then was *Oh, crap.*

In spite of that, she said, "No clue."

"Mr. *Hawthorne*," Grady said again. "We have to leave. *Now.* Explanations can wait."

"Actually, Inspector Grady," Tate said, returning his attention to him, "you won't have much to explain. I'm guessing you're here because my grandfather was Joseph Bacco, aka the Iron Don, and now that he's gone, he wants me to be the new Iron Don."

"You know about that?"

"I do."

Grady eyed him warily for a moment. "Okay. I wasn't sure you were even aware you had a WITSEC cover, if your mother ever made you privy to that or if you remembered that part of your life. The other thing I came here to tell you is that your WITSEC cover has been compromised, thanks to a hack in our files we discovered just this morning. We need to put you somewhere safe until we can get to the bottom of it."

Tate barely heard the second part of the marshal's comment. He was too focused on the first part. "You knew my mother?"

Grady was visibly agitated about his lack of compliance with the whole *leaving immediately* thing, but he nodded. "I was assigned to your father and his family after he became a state's witness. The last time I saw your mother or you was the day your father died."

Okay, *that* was why he looked familiar. The man in the suit that day must have been a younger Terrence Grady.

"Look, Mr. Hawthorne, we can talk about this in the car," he said. "We don't know that there's a credible threat to your safety, but we can't be sure there *isn't* one, either. There are an awful lot of people interested in taking over your grandfather's position—

the one they know your grandfather wanted you to assume—and it's safe to say that few of them have your best interests at heart. Last week, someone accessed your federal file without authorization, so your WITSEC identity is no longer protected. That means I have to get you someplace where you *are* protected. *Immediately.*"

"Um, Inspector Grady?" Renata said nervously. "I, uh… That is, uh… Funny story, actually…"

"Spit it out, Ms…" Grady said.

She began patting her bun again, but this time kept doing it the entire time she spoke. "Twigg. Renata Twigg. And, actually, the person who compromised Mr. Hawthorne's WITSEC identity? Yeah, that, um…that might have been, ah…me."

Grady eyed her flatly. "You're the one who told Mr. Hawthorne about his past?"

Something in his tone made Renata pat her bun harder. "Um…maybe?"

Tate was going to tell Grady that she absolutely had been the one to tell him about that, but he was kind of enjoying how her bun patting was causing strands of hair to come loose. Her hair was longer than it looked.

"You have access to federally protected files, have you?" Grady asked. "Or do you have hacking skills that allowed you to access those files? Because hacking a federal database is a Class B felony, Ms. Twigg. One that carries a sentence of up to twenty years."

She looked a little panicked by that. "Of course I don't have hacking skills," she said. "Are you kidding? I majored in English specifically so I wouldn't have to do the math."

"Well, which is it, Ms. Twigg?" Grady asked. "How did you discover Mr. Hawthorne's identity? And why did you go looking for him in the first place?"

She bit her lip anxiously. Tate tried not to be turned-on.

Quickly, she told Grady about Joey the Knife's will and his intentions for his grandson. Grady nodded as she spoke, but offered no commentary.

When she finished, he asked again, "And just how were you able to locate Mr. Hawthorne?"

At first, she said nothing. Then, very softly, she asked, "Class B felony, you say? Twenty years?"

Grady nodded.

For a moment, Renata looked like the proverbial deer in the headlights, right down to the fawn-colored suit and doe eyes. Then her expression cleared, and she said, "Craigslist."

Grady looked confused. Tate wasn't surprised. He'd been confused since seeing Renata at his front door.

"Craigslist?" Grady echoed.

Renata nodded. "I found a computer whiz on

Craigslist who said he could find anyone for any-body for the right price. He helped me locate Mr. Hawthorne."

"His name?" Grady asked. Dubiously, if Tate wasn't mistaken.

Renata briefly did the deer-in-the-headlights thing again. Then she told him, "John something, I think he said. Smith, maybe?"

Grady didn't look convinced. "And do you know if Mr., ah, Smith did anything else with this infor-mation he found for you? Like, I don't know…sold it to someone else besides you?"

"I'm sure he's totally trustworthy and kept it all completely confidential," Renata said.

Now Grady looked even less convinced. "A guy on Craigslist who says he can find anybody for any-one for money and calls himself John Smith is to-tally trustworthy," Grady reiterated. Blandly, if Tate wasn't mistaken.

Renata nodded with much conviction and re-peated, "Totally."

Grady looked at her for a long time, as if weigh-ing a number of scenarios. Finally he growled, "We don't have time for this right now. We need to get Mr. Hawthorne somewhere safe. And until it's all sorted out, you're coming, too, Ms. Twigg."

That finally stopped the bun patting. But it re-started the button fumbling. So much so that Renata actually undid the button, and then another below it, revealing a tantalizing glimpse of lace beneath. Which was weird, because in light of developments over the last several minutes, the only thing Tate should find tantalizing about Renata Twigg was thoughts of her having never entered his life in the first place.

"I'm sorry, but I can't go anywhere with you," she said to Grady. "I have a red-eye out of O'Hare tonight."

"You don't have a choice, Ms. Twigg," Grady said emphatically. He turned to Tate. "And neither do you. We're all leaving. Now. Once the two of you are settled in a safe house, we can get this all straightened out. But until we know there's no threat to Mr. Hawthorne, and until we get to the bottom of this security breach, both of you—" he pointed first at Tate, then at Renata "—are coming with me."

Three

Renny sat in the backseat of the black SUV with Tate, wishing she could wake up in her Tribeca condo and start the day over again. They'd been driving for more than two hours nonstop—pretty much due north, as far as she could tell—and Tate had barely said a dozen words to her during the entire trip.

He'd spoken to the marshal often enough early on—or, at least, tried to. Grady had responded to every question with a promise to explain once he was sure Tate and Renny were settled at a safe location. He'd replied the same way as he hustled the two of them out of the house earlier. He hadn't even

allowed Tate time to change his clothes, hadn't allowed Renny to bring her handbag or portfolio and
had made them both leave behind their electronics
due to their GPS.

On the upside, the fact that Grady hadn't allowed
them even basic necessities might be an indication he
didn't intend to detain them for long. On the down-
side, the fact that they were still driving after two
hours was a pretty decent indication that Grady
planned on detaining her and Tate for some time.

She just wondered how far from Chicago Grady
thought they had to be before they'd be considered
safe. They'd crossed the Wisconsin state line less
than an hour after leaving Tate's house and had kept
driving past Racine, Milwaukee and Sheboygan.
Like any good Northeasterner, Renny had no idea
which states actually abutted each other beyond the
tristate area, but she was pretty sure Wisconsin was
one of the ones way up on the map beneath Canada.
So they couldn't drive much longer if they wanted
to stay in Grady's jurisdiction.

As if cued by her thoughts, he took the next exit
off I-43, one that ended in a two-lane blacktop with
a sign indicating they could head either west to a
place called Pattypan or east to nowhere, because
Pattypan was the only town listed. In spite of that,
Grady turned right.

Okay then. Nowhere it would be.

The interstate had already taken them into a densely forested area, but the trees grew even thicker the farther they drove away from it. The sky, too, had grown darker the farther north they traveled, and the clouds were slate and ominous, fat with rain.

This day really wasn't turning out the way Renny had planned. She braved another look at Tate, who had crowded himself into the passenger-side door as if he wanted to keep as much space between them as possible. He wasn't turning out the way she'd planned, either. She was supposed to have gone to his house in her usual professional capacity, relayed the terms of his grandfather's will in her usual professional way and handled his decision, whatever it turned out to be, with professionalism.

Any personal arrangements Tate wanted to make with the Bacco family would have been up to him. Then Renny would have gone back to her life in New York having completed what would be the most interesting case she would ever handle in her professional career and try not to think about how early she'd peaked.

Instead, all her professional responses had gone out the window the moment she saw Tate, and every personal response had jumped up to scream, *Howdy do!* And those responses hadn't shut up since, not even when the guy was giving her enough cold shoulder to fill a butcher's freezer.

The SUV finally turned off the two-lane black-top, onto a dirt road that sloped sharply upward, into even more trees. The ride grew bouncy enough that Renny had to grab the armrest, but that didn't keep her from falling toward Tate when they hit a deep rut. Fortunately, she was wearing her seat belt, so she only slammed into him a little bit. Unfortunately, when they came out of the rut, he fell in the other direction and slammed into her, too.

For one scant moment, their bodies were aligned from elbow to shoulder, and Renny couldn't help thinking it was their first time. Um, touching, she meant. Arms and shoulders, she meant. Fully clothed, she meant. But the way her heart was racing when the two of them separated, and the way the blood was zipping through her veins, and the way her breathing had gone hot and ragged, they might as well have just engaged in a whole 'nother kind of first time.

She mumbled an apology, but he didn't acknowledge it. Instead, he gripped his armrest as if his life depended on it. After another few hundred jostling, friction-inducing feet of what may or may not have once been a road, the SUV finally broke through the trees and into a clearing.

A clearing populated by a motel that was clearly a remnant of mid-twentieth-century, pre-interstate travel culture—single story, brick and shaped like a giant L. There was a parking space in front of each room, but there wasn't a single car present. In fact, the place looked as if it had been out of business since the mid-twentieth-century, pre-interstate travel culture. The paint on the doors was peeling, the brick was stained with mold and a rusty, mottled sign in front read The Big Cheese Motor-Inn. In a small clearing nearby were a half-dozen stucco cottages shaped like wedges of cheese. It was toward one of those that Inspector Grady steered the SUV.

"Seriously?" Renny said when he stopped the vehicle and threw it into Park. "You're going to hide us in a cottage cheese?"

"We've used this place as a safe house since nineteen sixty-eight," Grady said. "That's when we confiscated it from the Wisconsin mob. These days, no one even remembers it exists."

"There's a Wisconsin mob?" Renny asked. "Like who? Silo Sal Schlitz and Vinnie the Udder?"

"There *was* a Wisconsin mob," Grady corrected her. "The Peragine family. Shipping and pizzerias."

Of course.

The marshal snapped off his seat belt, opened his door and exited, so Renny and Tate did, too. The moment she was out of the vehicle, she was swamped by heat even worse than in Chicago. Impulsively, she stripped off her jacket and rolled her shirt sleeves to her elbows. Her hair, so tidy earlier, had become a tattered mess, so she plucked out the pins, tucked them into her skirt pocket and let the mass of dark hair fall to the center of her back. Then she hastily twisted it into a pin-free topknot with the deftness of someone who had been doing it for years, drove her arms above her head and pushed herself up on tiptoe, closing her eyes to enjoy the stretch.

By the time she opened her eyes, Tate had rounded the back of the SUV and was gazing at her in a way that made her glance down to be sure she hadn't stripped off more than just her jacket. Nope. Everything was still in place. Though maybe she shouldn't have fiddled so much with her shirt buttons earlier, since there was a little bit of lace and silk camisole peeking out.

But come on. It was a camisole. Who thought camisoles were sexy these days?

She looked at Tate, who was eyeing her as if she were clad in feathery wings, mile-high heels and a two-sizes-too-small cubic-zirconia-encrusted bra. Oh. Okay. Evidently, there was still at least one guy in the world who found camisoles sexy. Too bad he also hated her guts.

As unobtrusively as she could, she rebuttoned the third and second buttons. Then she followed Grady to the giant cheese wedge, telling herself she only imagined the way she could feel Tate's gaze on her ass the whole time.

"Oh, look," she said in an effort to dispel some of the tension that had become thick enough to hack with a meat cleaver. "Isn't that clever, how they made some of the Swiss-cheese holes into windows? That's what I call functional design."

Unfortunately, neither man seemed to share her interest in architectural aesthetics, because they just kept walking. Grady pulled a set of keys from his pocket as he scanned the tree line for signs of God knew what, and Tate moved past her to follow the marshal to the front door, not sparing her a glance.

Renny deliberately lagged behind, scanning the tree line herself. Though for different reasons than Grady, she was sure. In spite of the weirdness of the situation, and even with the suffocating heat and teeming sky, she couldn't help appreciating the beauty surrounding her. The trees were huge, looking almost black against the still-darkening clouds, and there was a burring noise unlike anything she'd ever heard. She recognized the sound as cicadas—she'd heard them on occasion growing up in Connecticut—but here it was as if there were thousands of them, all singing at once.

The wind whispered past her ears, tossing tendrils of hair she hadn't quite contained, and she closed her eyes to inhale deeply, filling her nose with the scent of evergreen and something else, something that reminded her of summers at the shore. That vague fishy smell that indicated the presence of water nearby. If they really had traveled due north, it was probably Lake Michigan. She wondered if they were close enough to go fishing. She'd loved fishing when she was a little girl. And she'd always outfished her father and brothers whenever they went.

She listened to the cicadas, reveled in the warm breeze and inhaled another big gulp of pine forest, releasing it slowly. Then she drew in another and let it go, too. Then another. And another. Bit by bit, the tension left her body, and something else took its place. Not quite serenity, but something that at least kept her panic at bay. She loved being outdoors. The farther from civilization, the better.

She felt a raindrop on her forehead, followed by a few more; then the sky opened up and the rain fell in earnest. Renny didn't mind. Rain was hydrotherapy. The warm droplets cooled her heated skin and *tap-tap-tapped* on the leaves of the trees and the hood of the SUV, their gentle percussion calming her even more.

With one final breath, she opened her eyes. Tate stood inside the door of the cottage looking out at her, his expression inscrutable. He was probably wondering what kind of madwoman he was going to be stuck with for the rest of the day—maybe longer. Renny supposed that was only fair, since she was wondering a lot of things about him at the moment, too.

Like, for instance, if he enjoyed fishing.

As Tate gazed at Renata, so much of what had happened today became clear. The woman didn't even have enough sense to come in out of the rain.

He must have been nuts to have thought her professional, capable and no-nonsense. Then again, he'd also been thinking she didn't seem to want to be any of those things. Now he had his proof. Even when the rain soaked her clothing, she still didn't seem inclined to come inside.

On the other hand, her saturated state wasn't entirely off-putting. Her white shirt clung to her like a second skin, delineating every hill and valley on her torso. Just because those hills weren't exactly the Rockies—or even the Grassy Knoll—didn't make her any less undesirable. No, it was the fact that she'd disrupted his life and gotten him into a mess—then made a literal federal case out of it—that did that.

Actually, that wasn't quite true. She was still desirable. He just didn't like her very much.

He heard Grady in the cabin behind him opening and closing drawers, cabinets and closets, and muttering to himself. But the activity still couldn't pull his gaze from Renata in the rain.

Renata in the rain. It sounded like something by a

French watercolorist hanging in the Musée d'Orsay. But there she was, a study in pale shades, and if he were an artist, he would be setting up his easel right now.

She really was very pretty. Not in the flashy, showy, don't-you-wish-you-were-hot-like-me way that the women he dated were. Her beauty was the kind that crept up on a man, then crawled under his skin and into his brain, until he could think of little else. A quiet, singular, unrelenting kind of beauty. When he first saw her standing at his front door that morning, he'd thought she was cute. Once they started talking, and he'd heard her breathless, whiskey-rough voice, he'd even thought she was kind of hot—in a sexy-librarian way. But now she seemed remarkably pretty. In a quiet, unrelenting, French-watercolorist kind of way.

"Mr. Hawthorne?" he heard Grady call out from behind him, raising his voice to be heard over the rain pelting the roof.

Yet still Tate couldn't look away from Renata. Because she started making her way to the door where he stood. She stopped long enough to remove her wet shoes, then continued barefoot. The dark hair that had been so severe was sodden and bedraggled now, bits of it clinging to her neck and forehead, and the suit that had been so efficient looking was rumpled and puckered. Somehow, though, that just made her more attractive.

"Mr. Hawthorne?" Grady said again, louder this time.

"What?" Tate replied over his shoulder. Because now Renata was only a few steps away from him.

"Sir, I'm going to have to go into town for some supplies. This place hasn't been used for a while, and I didn't have any notice that we'd be needing it. I did turn on the hot-water heater, so there should be hot water in a few hours. But the place is kind of light on fresh food. I shouldn't be gone long."

Renata was nearly on top of Tate now—figuratively, not literally, though the literal thought was starting to have some merit. So he stepped just far enough out of the doorway for her to get by him, but not far enough that she could do it without touching him. She seemed to realize that, because she hesitated before entering, lifting her head to meet his gaze.

As he studied her, a drop of rainwater slid from behind her ear to glide down the column of her neck, settling in the divot at the base of her throat. He was so caught up in watching it, to see if it would stay there or roll down into the collar of her shirt, that he almost forgot she wasn't the kind of woman he found fascinating. It wasn't Renata that fascinated him at the moment, he assured himself. It was that

drop of rainwater. On her unbelievably creamy, flawless, beautiful skin.

When he didn't move out of her way, she arched a
dark eyebrow questioningly. In response, he feigned
bewilderment. She took another small step forward.
He stood pat.

"Do you mind?" she finally asked.

"Mind what?"

"Moving out of the way?"

Well, if she was going to speak frankly—another
trait he disliked in women—there wasn't much he
could do but move out of the way.

"Of course," he said. And moved a step as small
as hers to the side.

She strode forward at the same time, but she
moved farther and faster than he did so her shoulder
hit him in the chest, and they both lost their footing.
When Tate circled her upper arm with one hand, he
discovered Renata Twigg had some decent definition in her biceps and triceps.

Muscles were another thing he wasn't crazy about
finding on a woman. So why did finding them on Renata send a thrill of…something…shooting through
his system?

"Sorry," he said.

"No problem," she replied. In a breathless, whiskey-
rough voice that made him start thinking about sexy
librarians again.

She kept moving, but even after she was free of him, his palm was still damp from her clothing, and there was a wet spot on his shirt where her shoulder had made contact. Those would eventually dry up and be gone. What wouldn't leave as quickly were the thoughts circling in his brain that were anything but dry.

He watched her as she continued into the cabin, noting how the rain had soaked her skirt, too. The skirt whose length barely passed muster for proper office attire. The dampness made it seem even shorter—though it could just be Tate's overactive imagination making it do that—and it, too, clung to her body with much affection. Whatever Renata lacked in the front—and, really, no woman ever lacked anything up front—she more than made up for behind. The gods might have made her small, but they'd packed more into her little package than a lot of women twice her size.

"Mr. Hawthorne?"

Reluctantly, he returned his attention to Grady. The marshal was looking at him in a way that indicated he knew exactly where Tate's gaze had been, and if he were Renata's father, he'd be hauling Tate out to the woodshed.

"Did you hear what I said?" he asked.

"You have to go into town for some supplies," Tate replied. See? He could multitask just fine, listening to Grady with the left side of his brain while ogling Renata with the right.

"And I won't be gone long," Grady added as he made his way to the front door. "There's a phone in the bedroom, but if either of you uses it to call anyone other than me, this is going to turn into a *much* longer stay than any of us wants. Get it?"

"Got it."

"Good." Without another word, Grady exited.

Leaving Tate and Renata truly alone.

Four

Renny watched Inspector Grady leave, then scanned the cottage and decided things could be worse. The place was actually kind of cute in a retro, Eisenhower-era kind of way. The walls were paneled in honey-colored wood, and a fireplace on one side was framed by creek stone all the way around. Doors flanked it on each side, one open and leading to a bedroom and the other closed, doubtless a bathroom. The wall hangings were amorphous metal shapes, and the rugs were textile versions of the same. The furniture was all midcentury modern—doubtless authentic—with smooth wood frames and square beige cushions. On the side of the cottage opposite the fireplace was a breakfast bar and kitchenette, whose appliances looked authentic to the middle of the last century, too.

The decor reminded her of James Mason's house on top of Mount Rushmore in *North by Northwest*. Any minute now, Martin Landau ought to come sauntering in to mix up a pitcher of martinis for all of them. Of course, then he'd try to kill Renny and Tate the way he'd tried to kill Eva Marie Saint and Cary Grant, so...

"So," she said, turning to face Tate again, "pretty crazy day, huh?"

She had hoped to lighten the mood with the question. But he only glowered harder.

She sighed. "I'm sorry, okay? For like the hundredth time, I'm sorry. Will you please stop looking at me like I ruined your life?"

"You have ruined my life," he said. Still glowering.

"I have not!" she denied. "All I did was tell you the truth about your origins. *I'm* not the one who spawned you into an alleged mob family. *I'm* not the one who tried to make you an offer you couldn't refuse. The circumstances of your birth and your grandfather's wishes are facts of your life. They have nothing to do with me."

"Yeah, but the facts of my life you dumped on me

today have ruined the facts of my life that existed before. Before today, my life was fine and would have
remained that way if you'd stayed in New York. No,
better than fine. Before today, my life was perfect."

"No one's life is perfect," Renny said. "There's
always some—"

"My life was. Until you knocked on my door."

Well, technically, she had rung his doorbell, but
it probably wasn't a good idea to argue that point.
Not when they had so many others to argue instead.
Not that Renny wanted to argue. Tate obviously did.
And maybe, on some level, she deserved the dressing-
down he was about to give her.

Although she really should have thought of another phrase than *dressing-down*, since she was
pretty sure he'd been doing that to her long before
he discovered the reason for her visit. So maybe, on
some level, she deserved the tongue-lashing he was
about to give her.

Um, no, that probably wasn't a good phrase to
use, either. So maybe, on some level, she deserved
the, uh…harangue—yeah, that was it—that he was
about to give her.

He didn't disappoint.

"A few hours ago," he began, his anger barely in
check, "my weekend was going to be great. After
polo, I had a late lunch with some friends to tell
them about an opportunity that would have netted

us each a bundle. And tonight, I had a date with a gorgeous redhead."

Ha. Just as Renny suspected.

"Tickets for a show that's been sold out for months, followed by dinner at a restaurant where it's even harder to get a table. Then back to my place for a nightcap and hours of the obvious conclusion to a night like that."

Renny wasn't sure what bothered her more. That he assumed a woman would have sex with him just because he spent a zillion dollars on an evening out— even if it did sound like a supernice evening—or the fact that he was cocky enough to think he would last for hours. With a stunning redhead.

Okay, so maybe it was actually the stunning red-head that bothered her the most. And, okay, maybe the supernice evening, too, since the high point of Renny's weekend would have been a few episodes of *Bletchley Circle* and a bag of gummi bears.

Feeling a little haranguey herself, she said tartly, "Obvious conclusion to a night like that? So the two of you go back to your place to binge-watch British mysteries on Netflix all night? 'Cause that's what I consider an 'obvious conclusion' to a night like that."

She didn't bother to clarify that that was because (A) she generally spent her weekends alone lately, and (B) she really loved binge-watching British mysteries on Netflix.

He eyed her blandly. "Find yourself going out for evenings like that a lot, do you?"

"Sure. All the time." At least once a month. Okay, maybe more like once a year. Okay, maybe more like never. He didn't have to know that, either. "I'm sure you'll have a chance to make it up to the stunning redhead."

"Not when I can't call her and tell her I won't be there. I can't even give her the tickets to the show so she can go with someone else."

He wouldn't mind his girlfriend going to the play with someone else? Did that mean she really wasn't his girlfriend? And that he might maybe possibly perhaps be open to seeing someone else? Someone who *wasn't* a stunning redhead, but was more of an ordinary brunette and—

Oh, Renny, stop. You're embarrassing yourself.

It only meant the focus of his evening wasn't the woman he was with or where they were going or what they were doing. The focus of his evening was its obvious conclusion. Meaning Tate Hawthorne was a guy with a pretty face and a gorgeous body that housed a truly superficial brain. Renny hated guys like that.

Even if they did have pretty faces and gorgeous bodies.

"I'm sure she'll understand," Renny said, "once you get back and explain what happened."

He shook his head. "How do I explain something like this? It sounds like a bad movie."

"That I didn't write," she reminded him. "Don't blame me for this."

He slumped forward a bit, as if he'd been holding his entire body too tightly for too long. Then he crossed the room and folded himself into a chair by the fireplace.

"It's just been a lot to take in, you know?" he said.

Renny moved closer, opting for the sofa. Tate stared straight ahead, but his gaze was unfocused, as if he were seeing something other than a dated but really kind of charming venue. Since his question hadn't seemed to require an answer, she said nothing. Especially since he looked ready to answer it himself.

"I've always had a plan for my life," he said. "Even when I was a kid. After my dad died, my mom struggled so much to keep a roof over our head, and I wanted to grow up and make as much money as I could so she didn't have to worry anymore. So *I* wouldn't have to worry. I hate worrying. I never worry. Worrying is for people who don't know how to make life work for them."

He turned to Renny, and she braced herself for more scowling. Instead, he looked kind of…lost? Confused? Uncertain? All of the above? Whatever it was, it was unsettling, because until now, Tate hadn't been any of those things. On the contrary, he'd been the most cocksure person she'd ever met.

"But now I'm worried," he said. "And I don't know how to handle it. Does that ever happen to you?"

She wanted to tell him no. She'd always had a plan for life, too, even when she was a kid. Attend the same high school as her parents. Get her BA in English from Vassar like her mother and graduate from Harvard Law like her father. Then go to work at his firm, since both of her brothers had opted to work in finance, and Renny had been his last hope. Eventually marry some as-yet-nameless up-and-comer like herself. At some point, squeeze out the requisite kid or two and hire a nanny like the one she'd had. Send the offspring to the same schools with the same majors so they could go to work at Tarrant, Fiver & Twigg, too, and start the cycle all over again. It was the upper-class, suburban way. Blah, blah, blah. She couldn't remember ever planning a life that was anything else.

But she could remember *wanting* a life that was anything else. She could remember that pretty well.

In spite of that, she told Tate, "No. It doesn't happen to me. I don't worry, either."

And she didn't. Because there was no uncertainty in her life. She had a job that paid well and guaranteed her a career—provided she didn't keep screwing up. She owned her condo and car outright. She carried no debt. Even if she did lose her job, she had trust funds from both sides of the family that would allow her to live comfortably for the rest of her life. There wasn't any uncertainty in Renny's life. She really didn't have anything to worry about.

Except for those days when she felt as if she'd ended up where she was through no thought or decision of her own. Except for those days when she carried around a knot in her stomach that couldn't be anything but, well, worry.

Days kind of like today.

She pushed the thoughts away. They were silly. Her life was fine. And it would stay fine. Fine was... fine. It was. It was totally, totally...fine. There were a lot of people who would kill to have lives that were fine. No way was she in any position to worry.

"I shouldn't be worried, though, right?" Tate asked, still sounding worried. "There's no way I'm going to take over my grandfather's position. And I don't have to meet my cousins or aunts or uncles if I don't want to, do I? They'd probably just as soon I stay out of their lives, right?"

"Maybe," Renny said. "But maybe not. Especially since you don't want to inherit your grandfather's estate or take his place in the business. Once the Bacco sisters and their families know you're not a usurper, they might want to reconnect with you."

Hey, it could happen. Joey the Knife had put an

awful lot of importance on family, even family who had strayed. It was possible Tate's aunts still loved their brother as much as their father had. It was possible that, in spite of everything, they'd like to see how their little nephew turned out. A lot of things were possible at this point. When Tate remained silent, she said, "You have a lot to think about. Maybe being separated from your life for a few days will be a blessing in disguise. It will allow you to mull your options without your other daily distractions."

"A few days?" he echoed, sounding even more worried. "You think we'll actually be here for a few days?"

"I think it's pretty clear we're not going home tonight. Not if Inspector Grady had to go into town for supplies."

And not if Renny continued to hide the fact that she knew perfectly well who was responsible for the security breach that compromised Tate's WITSEC identity. She was no happier to be here than Tate was. But what was she supposed to tell Inspector Grady after he said hacking a federal database the way Phoebe had could land her in prison for twenty years? And probably Renny, too, as an accessory. She'd had no idea what to say at that point. She'd been too busy panicking. Tate wasn't the only person who had a lot to think about.

"You said 'a few days,'" he told her. "Not 'over-night.'"

"Well, it *is* the weekend," she said. "Not much gets done on Saturday or Sunday in the world of bureaucracy."

"So it could be Monday before we get the all clear?" he asked.

"Or maybe Tuesday," she hedged. "Everyone in Washington could be coming back to work after a weekend at the shore or something. Takes a while to get going again after a weekend like that. I mean, conceivably, it could even be Wednesday before we—"

"Wednesday?" he bellowed. "That's four days stuck here."

Well, only if they decided by then that the hack into the WITSEC system hadn't originated with someone in the Bacco family looking to off Tate to keep him from taking over his grandfather's position. Until someone at the Justice Department realized there was no danger to him—and Renny really, really hoped they could do that without discovering the true source of the hack—he and Renny could be stuck in this dated but really kind of charming venue for a while.

"I don't know," she said in response to his question. "We can ask Inspector Grady when he gets back how long he thinks we'll have to be—"

Out of nowhere, a crack of thunder shook the cottage, a burst of lightning flashed outside the windows and the single table lamp Grady had lit upon entry flickered off, then on again. It was only then that Renny realized how uncomfortably warm it had become inside.

"Mind a little air-conditioning?" she asked.

Tate still looked a little distracted—and a lot annoyed—but he shook his head. She glanced around for a thermostat, saw one by the front door and headed for it.

"It's only for heat," she said upon further inspection.

She checked the windows for an air conditioner. Nothing. She wandered into the bedroom, which was as retro as the living room—and which also had only one bed that didn't even appear to be queen-size—but there was no window unit in there, either.

Okay, so it was an old motel that was out of use, and it was Wisconsin, where maybe summers didn't usually get that hot, but still. It was hot. They'd just have to cool off the old-fashioned way. If nothing else, rain usually brought the temperatures down.

She returned to the living room and opened one of the windows in there...only to be pelted by rain, so she closed it again. Or, at least, she tried to. But it got jammed to the point where she was banging on the window sash with both hands as water streamed down her arms, making it too slippery to get the damned thing back in its groove.

Before she realized what was happening, Tate was behind her, leveraging his extra foot of height to wrestle the window back into place for her. He surrounded her completely, his entire body flush against hers, his front to her back, his arms over her shoulders, his legs pressed into her fanny. With every move he made—and he made a lot of them— he seemed to press closer still, until Renny felt as if he were crawling inside her. And still the rain came pouring in the window, drenching them both, doing nothing to cool her off. On the contrary, the air around them fairly sizzled as their bodies made greater contact, creating a blistering friction that made her feel as if she would spontaneously combust. Finally, Tate shoved the window back into place, leaving them both wet and panting and—

And *not* moving away from each other.

Five

In fact, Tate seemed to be moving closer still. And if Renny had thought it was hot and steamy in the cottage before, it was nothing compared to the way she felt with him surrounding her, clinging to her as snugly as her clothes. Good God, the man was tall. And broad. And hard. And hot. And—

And get a grip, Renny.

He was just a guy. Just a really sexy guy. With a beautiful face. And a gorgeous body. And millions—possibly billions—of dollars. Who, she was reasonably certain, didn't like her very much.

So why wasn't he moving away from her?

She discovered the answer when she tried to re-
treat first, by shifting her body to the right. The moment she did, she felt it—felt him—hard and ripe
and ready against her back. She wasn't the only one
who'd been affected by the friction of their bodies.
The evidence of Tate's reaction was just a lot more
obvious than her own, thanks to his anatomy. The
anatomy that, some other time, she would take a moment to appreciate but that, at the moment... Oh, all
right—she appreciated it now, too. What she didn't
appreciate were the circumstances that had brought
both their anatomies so close, in a situation where
they couldn't do anything about it.

In an effort to relieve the tension—or whatever—
they both must be feeling, she tried to move a little
farther to the right. But he dropped his hands from
the window to cup them over her shoulders.

"Don't," he said softly. "Just...don't move."

"But I—"

"Don't," he repeated, a little more roughly.

Reluctantly, Renny stopped, but she couldn't ignore the pressure of him behind her. For one long
moment, they stood still, utterly aware of each other.
Then, finally, he removed his hands from her shoulders. She waited for him to take a step backward,
but he stayed where he was, dropping his hands to
her waist, instead.

Okay, now he would move away—or at least move

her away from him. But neither of those things happened, either. Instead, he dipped his head closer to hers. She felt a warm percussion of breath stir her hair from behind, then heard the soft sigh of his exhalation near her ear.

Unable to help herself, she turned her head toward the sound, only to find her mouth hovering within inches of his. Her gaze flew to his, but he had his lowered. At first she thought he was studying her mouth, and then she realized his eyes were too hooded for that, and his focus was even farther down. What he was really looking at was... She bent her own head to follow his gaze. He was looking at her shirt. More specifically, he was looking down her shirt. At the hint of camisole lace that still peeked out of the neckline. But when she looked back up at him, he had shifted his attention again, and this time he was definitely looking at her mouth. Then he was looking at her eyes. Then her mouth again.

And then his head was lowering more, his mouth drawing nearer to hers...nearer...nearer still. Renny held her breath as she felt his hands on her hips inching forward, one up along her ribs and the other down across her belly. She realized belatedly that she was still clinging to the windowsill, something that gave him free rein over her midsection. He curved one hand under her breast and pushed the other over her skirt at the juncture of her thighs.

She spun around to face him, opening her hands over his chest to push him away. Though she didn't push very hard, and he didn't go very far, it was enough for her to regain some semblance of sanity, enough to remember she barely knew him—even if it somehow felt as if she'd known him forever— enough to remind herself he didn't like her.

"Stop," she said quietly. "Just…stop."

Although the admonition echoed his own warning of a moment ago, the fact that she still had her hands splayed open over his chest—oh, wait, her fingers were actually curled into the fabric of his shirt, as if she intended to pull him forward again—didn't exactly put a fine point on her objection.

Tate seemed to notice that, too, because he cupped his hands over her hips, pulled her close and asked, "Why? We're obviously attracted to each other. You said yourself we're going to be stuck here for a while. It would be a nice way to pass the time."

Oh, and wasn't that what every woman wanted to be to a really hot, really sexy guy with millions— possibly billions—of dollars? A way to *pass the time*? Where did Renny get in line to sign up for that?

She forced herself to let go of his shirt—it actually would be a nice way to pass the time if it weren't for that pesky *he doesn't like you* thing—and covered his hands with hers to remove them from her hips.

"It's not a good idea," she said.

He circled her wrists with deft fingers and moved both their hands behind her back, then leaned in again. "Oh, I think it's a *very* good idea."

He started to lower his mouth to hers, and, God help her, Renny stood still for the merest of seconds and waited for him to make contact. He was just so unbelievably…so extremely…so totally, *totally*…

His lips brushed hers lightly…once, twice, three times, four. Heat splashed in her belly, spilling through her torso and into her limbs, warming parts of her she hadn't even realized were cold. Then he stepped closer and covered her mouth completely with his, and those parts fairly burst into flame. For another scandalous, too-brief moment, she reveled in the fantasy that was Tate Hawthorne and the wild ride it promised. Then, nimbly, she tugged her hands free of his and somehow broke away to scurry to the kitchenette.

"Hey, are you as hungry as I am?" she asked when she got there.

Belatedly, she realized the glaring double entendre of the question. Because there was hunger, and then there was *hunger*. And, speaking for herself, anyway, she was feeling a lot more of the latter than she was the former.

In spite of that, she asked, "You want a sandwich? I could really go for a sandwich."

Then she remembered Grady had gone into town

for supplies, which meant there probably wasn't much in the cottage for a sandwich.

She spun around so she wouldn't have the temptation that was Tate Hawthorne making her want a lot more than a sandwich and opened the refrigerator. It was empty save for a couple of bottles of water and a six-pack, minus two, of Spotted Cow beer. The freezer held only a handful of indeterminate foil-wrapped things all covered with frost. She tugged on one of the cabinet doors and found plates and glasses. Another offered a near-empty roll of paper towels. Then, finally, she found some food in one. Lots of food, actually. Lots of canned food. Lots of canned food that might be as midcentury modern as everything else in the place. She pushed herself up on tiptoe to reach one in front and flipped it over to inspect the date on the bottom. Then she smiled.

"Gotta love preservatives," she said. "This will still be good when I hit the big three-oh."

There was a long stretch of silence, then an even longer sigh of resignation, then the scrape of Tate's boots across the floor.

"And when will that be?" he asked impassively.

His voice came from so close behind her Renny actually jumped. She spun about to find him doing the surrounding thing again, though this time at least he gave her a couple of inches of space that allowed for some air circulation that might dry her clothes and some thought circulation that might clear her head.

"Um, a year," she told him. "Well, a year and two months."

He looked surprised. "I thought you were fresh out of law school."

She was grateful for the change of subject and clung to it, even though the subject was her, a topic she normally avoided. Still, when the alternative was thinking—or, worse, talking—about the mind-scrambling kisses they'd just shared...

"Nope," she said. "I passed the bar six years ago. So... Beefaroni?" She held up the can for his inspection.

He grimaced. "Really? You'd eat that?"

She gaped at him. "It was only my favorite dish the whole time I was in lower school. Of course I'll eat it. It's delicious."

He looked past her into the cabinet. "What else is in there?"

She turned around and started sorting through the cans, fairly certain that none of them would compare to what he would have found on the menu of a Chicago restaurant where it was nearly impossible to get a table, which he would have been perusing this evening if he wasn't stuck in a giant wedge of cheese with Renny and Chef Boyardee.

"Let's see," she said. "There's SpaghettiOs, Mini

Raviolis, beef stew, baked beans, chili mac, a variety of soups... Anything sounding good?"

When she turned back for his reply, he somehow seemed even closer than he'd been before. Judging by the expression on his face, though, no, nothing sounded good. In fact, everything sounded revolting.

In spite of that, he asked, "What kind of soup?"

She turned to check. "Clam chowder, creamy potato, beef barley, chicken and stars—"

"Is it Campbell's chicken and stars?"

"Yep."

"Fine. I'll have that."

Before she could grab it, he reached over her head to pluck the can from the shelf. Then he moved to the stove to open the drawer beneath it and retrieve a serviceable saucepan. He turned the proper burner knob to medium high without even having to check which one it was, effortlessly popped the lid on the can and plopped its contents into the pan. His moves were quick and fluid, automatic enough to make it seem as if he made canned soup in a not particularly up-to-date kitchenette every day because he had one just like it at home in his ivy-encrusted, multimillion-dollar mansion.

The only thing he did wrong as far as Renny could tell was that he added only half a can of water to the condensed soup, instead of the full can she knew the directions called for. She knew that because chicken and stars had also been a fave of hers when she was a kid. Enough that she still bought it on a fairly regular basis and hid it in her cabinets behind the jars of organic tomatoes, the boxes of steel-cut oats, the tins of gourmet green tea and the bottles of extra-virgin, first cold-pressed olive oil. Right beside the cans of Beefaroni.

Anyway, she was just surprised he knew his way around a can of soup and an antiquated kitchen. Well, knew his way around an antiquated kitchen, anyway. As for the soup…

"You should add a full can of water," she said. "The directions call for—"

"A whole can," he finished in unison with her. "I know. But a whole can waters it down. A half can gives it more flavor."

Oh. Okay. So maybe he did know his way around a can of soup, too. It was still weird, because he seemed like the last kind of guy who would have even a nodding acquaintance with either.

As if he'd read her mind, he told her, "My mom and I lived on canned stuff for years when I was a kid. After my dad died, the two of us only had her income to live on. We made regular visits to the food bank. Almost everything there came in cans."

And a growing boy's hunger must have been voracious, she thought, filling in the blanks he didn't want to fill himself. Canned food probably barely made a dent in it. Maybe that was why he turned his nose up at canned stuff now. Because he'd paid his canned-food dues a long time ago. She honestly didn't know anything about him other than the name he'd been given from WITSEC and what she'd heard and observed today. She'd been so happy when Phoebe had sent her the info about him, something that prevented Renny from screwing up again—ha— that she immediately looked up his most recent contact info, got in touch with his assistant and booked her flight to Chicago. And when she'd seen his house, she just assumed he must have lived that way forever.

"Lower school," he said.

"What?" she asked.

"You said Beefaroni was your favorite food when you were in lower school. Not 'grade school.' You said, 'lower school.'"

It took her a moment to rewind their conversation back to where she had used the phrase. But she didn't understand the distinction he was making. "Yes. So?"

"So you must have gone to private school. Only private schools use that 'lower school' designation. Anywhere else, you would have said 'grade school.' Or 'elementary school.'"

And if Tate had grown up on canned food and his mother's solitary paycheck, then he must not have gone to private school. Renny wondered if he was one of those people who'd been so driven to succeed as an adult because he'd been so deprived as a child.

"I did go to private school, actually," she told him. Without elaborating. Since there was really no reason to rub his nose in her privileged upbringing when he'd had what must have been a pretty challenging one himself. Even if he was superrich now, no one ever left their childhood far behind. Renny knew that, because every time she had to spend more than five minutes with either of her parents, she immediately regressed into that five-year-old disappointment shedding her pink tutu.

Tate, however, seemed to want her to elaborate, because he asked, "Was it one of those really tony private schools with marble floors and mahogany paneling and farm-to-table lunches?"

"Um, kind of," she admitted. She figured it wasn't necessary to add that it had also sat on acres and acres of gorgeously manicured green space that lent itself to some really beautiful pastoral afternoons when they sometimes held classes outdoors.

Instead, she said softly, "I'm sorry about your dad."

He'd located a spoon—also in the first drawer he checked—and was slowly stirring the soup, gazing into it as if it might offer him the answers he needed to get out of this mess.

"It was a long time ago," he replied just as softly.

"I really don't remember him that well. My stepfather was more of a father to me than my dad was. Not that I'm saying my biological father was a bad father," he hastened to add, glancing up long enough to see if Renny had drawn the wrong conclusion. "Just…my stepfather is the only father I really knew, you know? My mom married him when I was ten. And he was a good guy. Good to my mom. Good for my mom."

Those last sentences—and Tate's absence from them—were awfully telling. Especially considering the way he'd sounded like a ten-year-old boy when he uttered them.

"Do you remember anything about your life before your parents went into the program?" she asked.

Still stirring the soup, he said, "A few impressions of isolated moments, but nothing that puts that life into perspective."

"And your mother never gave you any reason to think there was this secret past she and your father shared?"

He shook his head. "Nothing. I mean, she was an overprotective mother—wouldn't let me do a lot of the things I wanted to do. But lots of moms are like that. I just figured she was a worrier."

Renny could relate. Her mom had worried a lot about her, too. But the reason Melisande Desjardins Twigg had worried about her daughter was because she wasn't daughter-like enough. When her mother took her to the store to order Renny her first set of big-girl bedroom furniture, they'd gone straight to the French Provincial—sorry, that was *Provençal Français*—section. Renny had uttered something along the lines of "Ew, grody" and dragged her mother to the bunk beds and desks made out of much sturdier stuff. When Renny wanted to wear a suit—with pants—to her middle school graduation instead of the white dresses the other girls had to wear, her mother had about had a heart attack. And when Renny decorated her high school mortarboard with a quote from Tupac instead of the Swarovski crystals her mother suggested, well…

Suffice it to say Renny had a long tradition of giving her mother cause to worry. At least, that was what her mother had always thought. Anyway, she could kind of relate to Tate Hawthorne at the moment.

She tried again. "Is there any chance maybe—"

"Look, Renata," he interrupted. He stopped stirring the soup and met her gaze. "I know you're just trying to help, but right now there's so much going on in my head I don't know what to think about any of it. I'd really rather not talk about it, okay?"

Not talking about it was another thing Renny understood. Her family were the hands-down champs of not talking about stuff. So were most of her ex-boyfriends, come to think of it.

"Okay," she said. "I understand. Just…when you're done with that pot, do you mind rinsing it out? I'll use it when you're finished."

He gazed at her in silence for another moment, as if he wasn't sure how to reply to what should be a simple question. "Sure," he said finally. "No problem."

A phone suddenly rang with the shrill retro ringtone used by so many today—except this one was shriller and more retro. When it sounded again, she realized it was coming from the bedroom. She and Tate hurried in that direction, but Renny had the lead on him and made it through the door first. She followed the ringing to the other side of the bed, where a plastic rotary phone sat on the lower shelf of the nightstand. She sprang for it as it rang again, landing on her stomach on the mattress, and snatched up the receiver.

"Hello?" she said breathlessly.

"Ms. Twigg?"

For some reason, she was disappointed to hear Inspector Grady's voice at the other end of the line. Who had she expected it would be? Her mother? The Publishers Clearing House Giveaway people? Walter, the guy who'd dumped her three weeks ago after two dates—not that she'd minded much, since he'd been so, well, Waltery?

"Hi, Mr. Grady," she said.

She looked over her shoulder at Tate, only to find

that he looked a little disappointed, too. Maybe he'd been expecting a call from his stunning redhead. Then his gaze skittered away from her face and landed... Well, there was no way to deny it. He was staring at her ass. Again. She grabbed the phone and maneuvered herself into a sitting position. When his gaze wandered to her face again, she did her best to glower at him. In return, he only smiled. Knowingly.

"Ms. Twigg? Are you there?"

"I'm here, Mr. Grady."

"Look, there's been a little trouble," he began.

Oh, duh, she wanted to reply. Instead, she listened as he told her how almost immediately after he arrived in town, the roads were closed behind him from flash flooding, and how he wouldn't be able to make it back to the cottage tonight, but there was some canned food and other stuff in the kitchen, enough to get them through till tomorrow, and blah, blah, blah, blah, blah. Renny didn't register much after that except for how Grady would get back as soon as he could, and he was sure Tate and Renny would be fine until he did, since nobody was getting out of Pattypan, Wisconsin, tonight, and nobody knew where she and Tate were, anyway.

All she could do was keep repeating, "Uh-huh... uh-huh...uh-huh." When she hung up the phone, Tate was still staring at her from the doorway, now with an expression that demanded, *Well?*

Gingerly, she set the phone back in its cradle. Nervously, she moved around the bed to return it to the nightstand. Anxiously, she tried to rouse a smile.

And then, very quietly, she said, "So. Looks like you and I are going to be on our own tonight. You know how to play Snap?"

Six

A raucous crack of thunder woke Tate from a dream about Renata. Or maybe not, he reconsidered when he saw her sleeping in a slant of moonlight in the chair near the sofa where he lay himself. She looked so fey and otherworldly, a part of him wondered if he might still be asleep. Once the thunder rolled off, the cottage was oddly quiet and, save for that one sliver of silver that had found her, very dark. He could still be dreaming. Any minute, he could wake up in his bed at home, with a belly full of sushi and champagne and a tumbled redhead sleeping beside him, waiting for him to wake her and tumble her again.

But if he woke in his own bed, it would mean Renata really had been nothing but a dream. And that would mean he'd never stood behind her wrestling with a window and his libido as he inhaled great gulps of her, a combination of immaculate sweetness and earthy sexiness that had nearly driven him mad. It would mean he'd never brushed her lips with his and been startled by the explosion of heat that rocked him, a reaction he hadn't had to a woman since... Hell, he didn't think he'd ever had a reaction like that to a woman. If Renata was nothing but a dream, and he woke up back in his real life, safe and sound, then that would mean he was back in his real life, safe and sound.

But that was what he wanted, wasn't it? His real life before she'd shown up at his front door? So why was he suddenly kind of relieved to realize he wasn't dreaming at all?

Lack of sleep, he told himself. It made people think crazy things. The rain had still been coming down in torrents when he and Renata ate a dinner of canned pasta just before sundown. Which, in hindsight, he had to admit hadn't been half-bad. The dinner or the company. Renata's incessant yakking had become less annoying as the day wore on. Maybe because trying to keep track of what she was nattering about had kept Tate from having to think about all the things he still wasn't ready to think about. Like not being who he'd always thought he was. Like having a family, regardless of how sketchy their origins might be. Like how tempting Renata smelled and how weird she made him feel.

The last thing he remembered before falling asleep, he'd been flipping through a years-old copy of *Esquire*, unable to sleep thanks to the storm raging outside, and Renata had been curled up in her chair with a tattered paperback she'd pulled from a bookcase in the bedroom. Something by Agatha Christie. He'd been surprised by her choice. It was so old-fashioned.

The book lay facedown in her lap now. One of her hands was curved loosely over its spine, and the other was dangling by the side of the chair. Her head was leaning back in a way that offered a tantalizing glimpse of her neck but guaranteed she would have a wicked ache in it when she woke. In spite of that, he was hesitant to rouse her. She just looked so...

He studied her again, the elegant line of her jaw, the sweep of dark lashes on her cheeks, the lush mouth. And the errant tresses of hair that fell from her ragged topknot, curving around the gaping shirt collar that still revealed a whisper of lace beneath.

Well, there was just something about moonlight that suited her. Who was Tate to mess with that?

What time was it? Automatically, he looked around for his phone, then remembered he didn't have it with him. Which naturally reminded him he didn't have anything with him. How the hell was anyone supposed to survive without even the most basic necessities? Like a cell phone? He rose and prowled around the cottage until he located a clock in the bedroom, one of those old plastic ones with glow-in-the-dark radium numbers. It was 1:57 a.m., according to the radioactive yet once common appliance. How had anyone survived the mid-twentieth century, anyway?

And just how much longer were they going to be stuck in this time warp of a place? Maybe he should be concerned about the fact that Grady had left the two of them alone, but the storm had worsened a lot after he left, so Tate hadn't been that surprised when the marshal was waylaid by flooding. He'd been heartened by Grady's assurance that he would be back tomorrow. Until the storm continued to lash for hours and the road they'd driven in on turned into a mud slide. Considering the lousy condition it was in when it was dry, he hated to think about how hard it would be to drive up the thing now, even with four-wheel drive. He and Renata could be living out of cans for a while.

Just like when Tate was a kid. Great. The last thing he wanted was to be reminded of that time in his life.

He returned to the living room and saw that Renata hadn't budged. Tate, on the other hand, was wide-awake. He seldom slept more than five hours a night, but he normally fell asleep much later than he did tonight. There was little chance he would be nodding off again any time soon. Normally, when he couldn't sleep, he went downstairs to his office to work. There was always plenty of that to catch up on. Here, though…

Well, he wasn't much of a reader. Not Agatha Christie, anyway. And as nice as it was to watch Renata sleep, to do that for any length of time put him in creepster territory. What did a man do in the middle of the night when he was locked up indefinitely with a beautiful woman who also had nothing to do?

Other than that?

Shower. Yeah, that was it. After spending the day in his polo uniform, he wasn't feeling exactly springtime fresh. Then again, once he showered, he was going to have to change back into the clothes on his back, since he'd left his house with nothing but, well, the clothes on his back. But if there was food in the cottage, maybe there were other provisions, too.

He returned to the bedroom and switched on a lamp by the bed. In the closet, he found a couple of shirts—off-the-rack and 100 percent polyester, he noted distastefully—and one pair of trousers that was four sizes too big for him. The shirts were all too big, too, save for one with long sleeves, but if he couldn't find anything else, he could make do.

He had better luck with the dresser. There was a sweater unsuited to swamp weather, but also a white cotton T-shirt. In another drawer, he discovered a pair of blue jeans, even if they were as midcentury as everything else in this place. The denim was soft and faded, and they had a button fly. But they were only one size too big, which at least made them workable. And it would make them more comfortable while he had to go commando waiting for his boxers to dry after washing them.

Just to be sure, he riffled through the rest of the drawers, but the only other clothes he found were some unspeakably ugly men's pajamas and some giant Bermuda shorts. Looked like Renata was out of luck. Evidently, the overwhelming majority of people who had to go into protective custody were men. Large men, at that.

Tate thought again about his parents. What had it been like for them, leaving everything behind and moving to a place they'd never visited before, having no clue what the future held? As bad as it was being stuck here with nothing, he at least knew that at some point he would be going back to his life and all that was familiar. His parents had had to build a new life in a new place with strangers they'd probably taken a long time to learn to trust—if they'd ever learned at all.

For some reason, that made him think again of Renata. In the moonlight. Looking soft and bewitching.

Shower, he reminded himself. He'd been about to take a shower. A nice, *long* shower. A nice, long, *cold* shower. He'd figure out the rest of it later.

Renny wasn't sure what woke her up. She only knew she was in semidarkness and wasn't in her own bed. When she lifted her head, her gaze fell on the book in her lap. Right, she recalled groggily. She was in King's Abbot with the recently deceased Roger Ackroyd. No, that wasn't right. She was in Wisconsin with Agatha Christie. No, that wasn't it, either. She was in Wisconsin with…

Tate Hawthorne. Right. It was all coming back to her now.

She rubbed her aching neck and sat up straighter, twisting to alleviate another ache in her back. Next time she fell asleep, it was going to be in bed. Then she remembered there was only one bed in the cottage. One bed that wasn't even queen-sized. Of course, there was also a sofa. Which didn't look very comfortable, the reason she'd chosen the chair for her reading.

Well, that and because Tate had been on the couch, surrounded by his cone of silence.

She heard what sounded like a metallic squeak, followed by the cessation of a humming she hadn't noticed until then, one she recognized as water rushing through pipes. Tate was in the shower. Or, more correctly, Tate was getting out of the shower. All naked and wet, and wet and naked, and covered in naked, wet skin. Like she really needed to have that information.

Thankfully, the only shower was in the bathroom adjacent to the bedroom, so he wouldn't come popping into the living room out of the other one all naked and wet, fumbling with a towel he couldn't quite get knotted around his waist, so it kept dipping low over his hips, under his flat waist and sculpted abs, low enough to reveal those extremely intriguing lines men had over their legs that curved and dipped down under the towel to frame what was sure to be a seriously impressive—

Anyway, that wouldn't be happening. For which Renny was exceedingly grateful. Really, she was.

She heard the bathroom door click open in the bedroom, and only then realized the reason the living room wasn't totally dark was because of the lamplight spilling in from that room. A great fist seized her insides and squeezed hard at the thought of Tate in there naked. She told herself she only imagined the scent of pine that seemed to permeate the entire cottage or the way the air suddenly turned all hot and damp. Then she heard the soft sound of bare feet on wood floor. She felt Tate moving closer behind her, then closer, then closer still.

She sat silently as he passed her chair—oh, yeah, that was definitely him causing the hot, steamy, piney thing—and seated himself on the couch. There was just enough light for her to see him, dressed now in a white V-neck T-shirt and faded blue jeans, a towel draped around his neck that he was using to scrub his close-cropped hair. She wondered where he'd found fresh clothes.

As if she'd asked the question aloud, his head snapped up, and his gaze met hers. "You're awake," he said.

"And you're clean," she replied, trying not to sound jealous. As uncomfortable as she'd been all day, it hadn't occurred to her to look for fresh clothes and get cleaned up. "You even shaved."

He lifted a hand to his beautiful jaw. "There are some disposable razors in the bathroom. If you're careful, you won't flay yourself alive with one. And there are some clothes in the bedroom that must have been left behind by previous visitors. A little big, but not too bad."

No, not too bad at all. As sexy as Tate had been in a skintight polo uniform, it was nothing compared to the jeans and T-shirt. Mostly because jeans and T-shirts were Renny's favorite attire for men. And when that T-shirt was V-necked enough to hint at the dark scattering of hair and sculpted muscle beneath, well…

"I don't suppose there was anything in my size, was there?" she asked in an effort to steer her brain in a new direction. "Something cute and comfy by Johnny Was, perhaps? Maybe some Tory Burch tomboy? Or some off-the-rack geek chic? I'd even settle for some sporty separates if they don't smell like swampland."

Because it was just Renny's luck to be trapped in the middle of nowhere with a rich, gorgeous, recently wet and naked playboy, and wearing the kind of clothes her mother would wear—which could only be made more off-putting by the added accessory of eau de quagmire.

Tate looked at her blankly. "The only part of that I understood was the word *tomboy*. If your definition of tomboy is men's shirts, trousers and pajamas that would swallow you, then, yeah. Have at it. Otherwise, the pickings are slim. But you might be able to figure out something."

Great. She could exchange clothes her mother would wear for clothes her father would wear. That was sure to make her less off-putting. Still, they would at least be clean and not stinky.

She looked at Tate again. At the curve of biceps peeking out from beneath the sleeve of his shirt. At the strong column of his throat. At the chiseled jaw now freshly shaved. And suddenly a shower seemed like a very good idea.

"Is there still some hot water?" she asked. Not that she would be using any hot water. Ahem.

"Oh, there's plenty," he said in a way that made her think he hadn't used any hot water, either. Hmm.

Without another word, she made her way to the bedroom. Tate's discarded polo uniform was folded loosely on the dresser, and his boots were on the floor below them. Quickly, she studied her apparel options in the closet and dresser, only to discover they were every bit as grim as he'd described. A gigantic man's shirt in the closet—in lavender, so apparently some criminals weren't afraid of a little color—would fall to her knees. But that was good, since she would have to wash out her underwear and let it air-dry, and she'd need something to cover her until then.

It took a minute for the significance of that to settle into her brain, and it only did because she walked into the bathroom to see a pair of men's silk boxers slung over the towel rack, drying. If Tate's underwear was hanging in here, then what was he wearing under his blue jeans out—

There was no way Renny was going to let herself think any further about that. Or about how she would have to go panties-free herself, wearing nothing but a gigantic men's shirt that could easily be brushed aside for a quick—

Well, all righty, then. The less gigantic men's pajamas it would be. At least she could—probably—keep them hitched up by tying a knot in the waistband. A really tight knot. That would be virtually impossible for Tate *or* her to get untied.

Yeah. That's the ticket.

She snagged those from the dresser drawer—they were bilious green and patterned with little golf carts—escaped to the bathroom, closed and locked the door, turned the cold faucet handle to full blast, and stripped off her fetid clothing. So she and Tate would be without underwear for a few hours. So what? People went without underwear all the time in some parts of the world, and they did just fine.

She stepped into the cold shower and yelped.

Oh, yeah. That should do it. For now, anyway.

Seven

Tate heard a yelp from the bathroom and figured Renata was having a close encounter of the cold-shower kind much like his own. Obviously, he wasn't the only one who was thinking about the repercussions of two red-blooded adults who'd been dancing around an attraction to each other all day, being left alone for the night with no underwear.

Well, okay, maybe they hadn't been dancing around it the entire day, since he still couldn't shake the memory of that too-brief embrace. The question now was, had Renata opted for the obnoxious pajamas in the dresser, or one of the shirts in the closet? 'Cause the latter would make things infinitely easier.

Suddenly feeling restless, he rose and padded barefoot to the kitchen, forgetting until he opened the refrigerator that there wasn't much there to keep his mind off what Renata might or might not be wearing. Automatically, he grabbed one of the beers and twisted off the cap with a satisfying hiss. Then he enjoyed an even more satisfying swallow. As good as it tasted, though, it wasn't enough to keep his thoughts from wandering back to Renata. Who, at that very moment, was standing naked beneath a rush of water under the same roof he was.

He couldn't remember the last time he'd been this close to a naked woman when the two of them weren't taking advantage of that. Then again, Renata wasn't exactly his type, he reminded himself. Again. She was the last kind of woman he needed or wanted in his life. He'd survived a lot of women who showed up regularly on those "toxic types to avoid" lists—the diva, the control freak, the drama queen and his personal favorite, the material girl. But he'd never had a run-in with a member of Renata's tribe: the walking disaster.

And that one was probably the worst of the bunch for a man like him. The other types could be handled once a guy figured out which of their buttons to push or not push and where and when they liked best to be stroked. But the walking disaster? There were too many buttons with that type, and stroking the wrong part could be catastrophic. With a woman like that, there were too many things outside a man's control. Too many things that could go wrong. As had been the case with Renata from nearly the moment she'd walked into his life.

Okay, so maybe she wasn't responsible for the circumstances of his birth and had nothing to do with his biological family being a *famiglia*. She was still a disaster. There were still too many variables with her. There was still so much that could go wrong. And don't even get him started on her buttons.

He heard the click of the bathroom door and glanced at the bedroom in time to see a shadow fall across the bed. She turned off the bathroom light and, before exiting it, the bedroom light, as well, throwing the entire cottage into darkness.

He heard the whisper of bare feet, followed by a softly uttered "Ow, dammit" as she slammed something that sounded a lot like her knee into one of the tables by the sofa. Finally, she snapped on the lamp and threw the living room into warm golden light.

Okay, maybe she wasn't quite a walking disaster. Maybe she was more of a moseying disaster. She was still someone he needed to avoid.

Which was going to be even harder now than it had been before, because Renata looked... Even with her hair wrapped up in a towel like a suburban-dwelling, SUV-driving spa-goer, she looked... Even in ugly men's pajamas that would fit three of her, she looked...

Wow. Renata looked really, really... Wow.

"Sorry about that," she muttered as she steadied the lamp on the table. "I'm not so good in the dark."

Oh, Tate doubted that. She'd done pretty well in the dark so far. He'd love to see how well she did other things in the dark.

"No worries," he said.

No worries. Right. She'd rolled up the legs of the pajamas to her knees, and the sleeves to her elbows, meaning she was covered just fine, but was also intriguingly...not. And even with every button of the shirt fastened, the deep V of its placket and collar meant the garment was open to the center of her chest.

Tate was suddenly, oddly, grateful she wasn't better endowed. At least this way, he could pretend there wasn't a luscious woman underneath those little golf carts. A luscious woman who could make ugly golf-cart pajamas sexier than the skimpiest lingerie.

Renata smiled shyly at him—*shyly*, when he was thinking about things like barely there lingerie and even more barely there pajama necklines—and then, still wearing her terry-cloth turban, she moved back to her chair and picked up the book she'd left lying there. Then she thumbed through the pages until she found the one where she'd left off. And then, *then*, she did something really remarkable.

She continued with her reading. As if nothing had changed in the few minutes since she emerged from the bathroom in a cloud of prurience and pine soap and potential developments.

Fine. Two could play at that game.

"Beer?" he asked.

She threw him another sweet smile and shook her head. "No, thanks. I'm good."

Then she went back to reading. With her head still wrapped in a towel. And ugly golf-cart pajamas hiding every interesting part of her—except that tantalizing bit of skin between her breasts that had become even more tantalizing by how the shirt now gaped open enough to reveal she was better endowed than he'd first thought.

He moved back to the sofa and picked up the magazine he'd already flipped through. He was about to remark on the editorial about whatever the hell it was about when she tented her book in her lap and reached up to unwind the towel on her head. After that, he couldn't remember much of anything, because her dark hair came tumbling out and spilled around her shoulders in ropes of damp silk.

He watched as she scrubbed her scalp with the towel, something that shouldn't have been sexy but which was unbelievably sexy. Then she draped the towel over the arm of the chair and began to comb her fingers through her hair. Okay, that was something that normally would be sexy—if the woman doing it wasn't wrapped in little cartoon golf carts—but with Renata, it was seriously sexy. Even in little cartoon golf carts. Maybe because of the way the top of the pajama shirt was opening and closing in time with her movements. Or maybe because of the way strands of her hair were clinging to her neck and chest the way Tate wanted to be clinging himself. Or maybe because it was nighttime, and the two of them were stranded here alone, and neither of them was wearing underwear.

Ah, dammit. He'd hoped he wouldn't think about that again.

Did that even matter, though? What Renata was doing was sexy, period. And it was sexy because she was sexy. Hell, at this point, the cartoon golf carts were even sexy. And if Renata gave him the smallest indication that she was thinking about the same things he was thinking about at the moment, then there was nothing that could stop them from—

"Um, Tate?" she asked suddenly. Softly. In a *very* intimate voice.

He did his best to sound noncommittal. "Yes, Renata?"

"Could you… Would you… I mean, I was wondering if you would mind if… I was wondering if you would, um…"

Whatever her very intimate question was, she couldn't seem to finish it. Which naturally made Tate think it was something really, *really* intimate. Something that obviously involved him, too. In a way she wasn't able to put into words, so she was relying on that very intimate tone of voice to convey her very intimate thoughts.

Her very intimate desires?

In an effort to help her along, he assured her, "Whatever you want to do, Renata…whatever you want *me* to do… I promise that I not only could do it, I would do it. I wouldn't mind at all, and I definitely would."

She smiled at his thorough answer to her very intimate question. At least one of them could make clear what was going on in his head. Women were just so damned circuitous.

Slowly, she stood, pushing her mass of dark hair over her shoulder. Then she took a step forward, toward Tate. He tossed aside the magazine, set his beer on the table and sat up for whatever she planned to do. He was about to lift his arms to pull her into his lap when she spun around and, without a word, headed back to the bedroom.

Well, okay, then. He hadn't pegged her as the sort of woman who would want to skip foreplay and get right to the main event, but hey, whatever. He aimed to please. Even if he did actually enjoy foreplay. Maybe next time. Or the time after that. Or the time after that. As she'd said, they could be here a few days.

He followed her to the bedroom only to discover she'd gone into the bathroom and closed the door. Maybe she was shy about undressing in front of him. Not that a woman who had just blurted out that she wanted to have sex should have been shy about anything, but...whatever.

He turned down the bed and switched on the lamp beside it, unleashing a veritable desert sun onto the bed. Well, hell. That wouldn't do. He liked to see what he was doing when he was with a woman, but he didn't want to be blinded while he was doing it. He flicked the switch again, but the lamp in the living room was as dim as the one in here was bright and barely reached the bed.

He remembered finding candles and matches in the kitchen when he was looking for a can opener. They were the stumpy white emergency kind, but they'd do. As quickly as he could, he collected them and returned to the bedroom, setting two on the dresser and two on the nightstand, then lit them all. Once they were going, he stripped off his shirt and went to work on the buttons of his fly.

He'd reached the last one when the bathroom door

opened and Renata emerged, her attention focused on something in her hand she was drying with her towel.

"I really appreciate this, Tate. My hair is just so unmanageable when it's this wet, and there's no hair dryer in this place. It's always a lot easier if someone else brushes it for me. I couldn't find a brush, but I found this comb, and it has wide enough teeth that it should work okay, but I wanted to wash it first, natch, and—"

She stopped in her tracks—and stopped chattering, too—when she saw him standing shirtless and nearly pantsless with the bed unmade behind him and candles burning beside it. "What the...?" she muttered.

"I thought you wanted to have sex," he said.

She expelled a single, humorless chuckle. "No."

She was so emphatic, the two-letter response actually came out with two syllables as *no-oh*. Then, as if he hadn't already figured out how emphatically she was saying no, she hastily clarified, "I want you to comb my hair."

"But you sounded like you wanted to have sex," he persisted, his testosterone, at least, not willing to give up the fight.

She gazed at him, mystified. "What about anything I said could have possibly sounded like I wanted to have sex?"

He replayed their conversation in his head. "Um, all of it?"

She was silent for a moment, but looked thoughtful enough that he could tell she was replaying the conversation in her head, too. For another hopeful moment, he thought she'd reply, *Oh, yeah. I guess I did sound like I wanted to have sex. Okay. Let's have sex!* Then her expression went confused again.

"There is no way you could have mistaken any of that for me wanting to have sex."

Fine. Tomatoes, tomahtoes.

He countered, "Well, I sure as hell couldn't tell you wanted me to comb your hair."

She said nothing for another moment, then, very quietly, asked, "Could you please button up your pants?"

Tate didn't think he'd ever had a woman ask him that question before. And, truth be told, it kind of startled him to hear it now. He'd just never had a woman turn him down. Ever. Even before he'd become the success he was now, with all the showy plumage of cars and cash and castle. When he was a college student living in a dump of a loft, he'd still always had girls over, whenever he'd asked. Hell, when he was in high school, driving a beat-up Ford Falcon, his backseat had seen constant action. Women had just always flocked to him, from the time he was old enough to want them to.

Except for Renata Twigg.

His gaze still fixed on hers, he began to rebutton his jeans. And he could barely believe his eyes when she actually turned her head to keep from watching him. How could a woman who inspired such abject wantonness in a man be too shy to watch him put himself back together? Especially when he hadn't even been completely undone?

"Thank you," she said when he'd finished. Still not looking at him, she added, "Now could you put your shirt back on, too?"

He bit back a growl of irritation as he grabbed the T-shirt from the bed and thrust it back over his head.

"Thank you," she said again.

But she still wasn't looking at him. Jeez, was he that unappealing?

Then he remembered she hadn't found him unappealing that afternoon. She'd melted into that kiss with as much appetite as he had. Even when she told him it wasn't a good idea for them to continue, she'd been clinging to his shirt as if she wanted to pull him back again. And the look in her eyes… There was no way a man could mistake a look like that. Since then, more than once, he'd caught her eyeing him in a way that made him think—no, made him *know*—she liked what she saw when she looked at him.

So it wasn't that Renata didn't want him the same way he wanted her. It was that she didn't want to want him the same way he wanted her. Which actually just confused him even more.

Women were weird. Why was sex such a big deal to them?

"So I guess this means you won't help me comb out my hair, huh?" she asked quietly.

He'd forgotten that was what she'd asked him to do. Then he surprised himself by saying, "No, this doesn't mean that."

Because, in spite of her not wanting to want him, Tate still wanted her. He had no idea why. Even if no woman had ever rebuffed him before, he wasn't the kind of guy to keep after one who did, regardless of her reasons. But he still wanted to be close to Renata. He still wanted to touch her. He still wanted to inhale great intoxicating gulps of her scent. And if combing her hair would bring him close enough to do those things, he was content to do it.

He sat on the bed and patted the empty place beside himself. "Sit down," he said. Then he held out his hand. "Give me the comb."

She studied him warily, then took a small step forward and handed him the comb. He took it without hesitation, then patted the seat beside him again. She took another step, one that brought her close enough for him to tumble her to the bed if he wanted. Which he did want. But she didn't. So he only patted the mattress one last time.

Finally, she sat, the bed giving enough beneath her to send her leaning his way. Her shoulder bumped his, but she ricocheted off and turned her back. After thrusting two big handfuls of hair over her shoulders, she mumbled another breathy thank-you and waited for him to begin. Tate lifted the comb to her long, dark, sexy hair and, as gently as he could, began to tug it through the mass.

Eight

Boys were weird.

As Renny sat on the edge of the mattress with her back to Tate, she tried to focus on that thought and not the other one attempting to usurp it about how good it felt to have his fingers running through her hair. That first thought made a lot more sense than the second did, anyway. Boys were weird. Men were even weirder.

All they ever thought about was sex, and everything had some kind of sexual component to it. There was no way Tate should have thought she was talking about sex when she was talking about hair combing.

She hadn't said a single word that was suggestive. On the other hand, it did feel kind of sexy the way he was combing her hair...

He was surprisingly gentle, cupping one hand tenderly over the crown of her head as he carefully pulled the comb along with small gestures. When he finished one section of hair, he pushed it forward over her shoulder and moved to another to start again. Her scalp warmed under his touch, a sweet, mellow heat that gradually seeped downward, into her neck and over her shoulders, then lower still, along her arms and down to the middle of her back.

"You're good at this," she said softly, closing her eyes.

He said nothing for a moment, then replied, just as softly, "Let me know if I hurt you."

"No worries," she quickly assured him.

Renny stopped thinking and just let herself feel. With her eyes closed, her other senses leaped to the fore. She heard the steady patter of rain on the window, smelled the clean scent of pine soap enveloping them. But most of all, she savored the warmth of Tate's palm on her head and the brush of his fingers along her neck, down her back and up again, as he untangled one strand of hair and moved it over her shoulder, followed by another. And another. And another. Again and again, his hand stroked her from her head to her waist, until all of her hair was streaming over her left shoulder, and the right side of her neck lay exposed.

By then, she felt like a rag doll, boneless and limp, her entire body evanescing into a state of serenity. Although he'd finished his task, Tate still sat behind her, and Renny said nothing to encourage him to move. On the contrary, she kind of wanted him to stay there forever, because even the slightest shift in their positions might ruin the sense of well-being that had come over her, a feeling that nothing in the world could ever go wrong again.

So lovely was the feeling that it seeped from her inside to her outside, manifesting as the brush of soft kisses along her neck and shoulders. Then she realized it wasn't she who was creating the sensation. It was Tate. He was dragging butterfly-soft openmouthed kisses over her sensitive flesh, pushing aside the fabric of her shirt as he went, stirring her already-incited senses to even greater awareness. On some level, she knew she should tell him to stop. But on another level, that was the last thing she wanted him to do.

"Tate," she murmured, still not sure what she wanted to say.

"Shh," he whispered, the soft sough a warm rush against her skin.

She opened her mouth to object again, but he nipped her shoulder lightly, igniting a blast of heat in her belly that flared into her chest and womb. She cried out softly in response, so he placed a soft kiss on the spot, tasted it with the flat of his tongue and peppered her shoulder with more caresses. Somewhere in the dark recesses of her brain, an alarm bell rang out, but the roar of blood in her ears deafened her to it. Especially when he roped an arm around her waist and pulled her back against himself, nuzzling the sensitive place behind her ear before dropping a kiss to her jaw.

It had been so long since she had enjoyed this kind of closeness with another human being. So long...

Too long.

Unable to help herself, Renny arced one arm backward, to skim her fingers through his hair. It was all the encouragement Tate needed. The hand at her waist rose higher, curling over her breast, thumbing the sensitive peak. She cried out again at the contact, the sound fracturing the stillness, and arched her body forward. Deftly, he unbuttoned her shirt and pushed the garment open, then cupped both hands over her naked breasts, kneading softly, rolling her nipples beneath his fingers. She gasped at the heat that shot through her and tried to turn to face him.

"Not yet," he whispered somewhere close to her ear.

She reached her other hand back to join the first, linking her fingers at the nape of his neck. Tate continued to stroke her breast with one hand as he dipped the other to the waistband of her pajamas. He effortlessly found the knot she'd tied in the side to keep them up, and just as effortlessly untied it. Then he dipped his hand beneath the fabric and between her legs, finding the feminine heart of her.

"Oh, God, you're already so wet," he murmured as he slid a finger inside her.

She gasped again, pushing her hips forward. He met her eagerly, driving his finger deeper, then sliding it out to furrow it between the hot folds of her flesh. Slowly, slowly…oh, so slowly…he caressed her, drawing intimate circles over her before pushing in and out of her again. He fingered her for long minutes, a hot coil inside her winding tighter and tighter as he did, until she feared she would explode from the sensations. Her breathing became more ragged, her pulse rate leaped and just when she thought she would come, he removed his hand and drew it upward again, laying it flat against her naked belly.

"Not yet," he whispered again.

In the candlelight, she felt more than saw him slip her shirt from her shoulders and toss it to the floor. But she couldn't help watching when he stood to remove his, too, reaching behind himself to grab a fistful of white cotton and drag it forward over his head. Beneath it, he was an awesome sight, muscle and sinew corded into a torso that could have been wrought by the hands of a Greek god. His biceps bunched as he undid the buttons of his fly one by one, until his blue jeans hung open on his hips, his member pushing hard against the soft denim. Then he joined her again on the bed, urging her toward the mattress until she was on her back and he was atop her, bare flesh to bare flesh. And then his mouth was on hers, consuming her, and it was all Renny could do not to come apart at the seams.

He touched her everywhere as he kissed her. He skimmed his palm along her rib cage, then into the narrow dip of her waist, then over her hip, down to her thigh and back again. Every time his hand moved over her, her pajama bottoms dipped lower, until he was tugging them out from under her and tossing them to the floor, too. And then Renny lay beneath him naked, feeling wanton, scandalous and aroused.

She explored Tate, too, running her hands over the bumps of muscle in his shoulders and arms, splaying her fingers wide over the silky skin of his back, dipping her hands beneath the loose denim on his hips to cup his taut buttocks. There wasn't an inch of him that wasn't hot and hard, especially when she guided her hand between their bodies and into his jeans to curl her fingers around his heavy shaft. He gasped at the contact, tasting her deeply and moving his hand between her legs again.

For long moments, they petted each other, matching their rhythm in languid strokes that gradually grew more demanding. As Renny drew near the precipice of an orgasm again, Tate suddenly pulled away, standing at the side of the bed.

With a devilish grin, he hooked his fingers in the waistband of his jeans and urged them down, until he was naked, too, gilded in the warm candle glow.

And if Renny had thought him an awesome sight before, now he was spectacular.

He moved back to the bed, sitting on its edge and pulling Renny into his lap to face him, straddling him. She guided her hands to his hair, stroking her palms over the silky tresses, loving the feel of having him so close. When he ducked his head to her breast, sucking her nipple deep into his mouth, she cried out again. And when he tucked his fingers gently into the elegant line bisecting her bottom to gently trace it, she gasped. But when he moved his hard shaft toward the damp, heated center of her, she drew herself backward, covering him again with her hand to halt his entry.

She couldn't quite bring herself to tell him to stop, though. She didn't want him to stop. She wanted him. A lot. It had been so long since she'd enjoyed this kind of release. It felt so good to be with him. And he was the kind of man she would never meet again. Why shouldn't she have one night with him? Where was the harm?

Oh, right. They'd had to leave without even the most basic essentials. Like, for instance, birth control.

"I want you, Renata," Tate said, his voice low and erotic, his hot gaze fixed on hers. "I really, really want you."

"I want you, too," she said. "But this is happening so fast, and I didn't exactly come prepared."

Boy, talk about a double entendre. Especially since she was less concerned about the birth control aftermath of a night like this than she was the emotional aftermath. She was at a place in her cycle where pregnancy was extremely unlikely, and her lady parts worked like clockwork. Would that she could be as confident that other parts of her body—like her heart—were as predictable.

"I didn't come prepared for a party, either," he told her. "But that doesn't mean we can't still have fun."

Before she could say any more, he dragged his fingers against her again, catching the sensitive nub of her clitoris gently between his thumb and middle finger. Renny gasped as he caressed her, heat rocketing through her body, pooling in her womb, driving all coherent thought from her brain. When he drove his finger into her again, she knew it would never be enough. She wanted more of him. She wanted all of him. She needed him inside her. Now. Her body demanded it.

That could be the only explanation for why she told him, "I won't get pregnant, Tate. The timing is completely wrong. And I want you inside me. Please. Make love to me. Now."

It was all the encouragement he needed. He pulled her close again, pressing his mouth to hers. Then he lifted her over himself and pulled her down, entering her slow and long and deep. When she opened her legs to accommodate him, he pushed hard against her, filling her, widening her even more. All she could do was wrap her arms around his neck and hang on for the ride.

And she rode him well, rising and falling on him, his shaft going deeper inside her with each new penetration. He moved his mouth to her breasts, cupping his other hand over her bottom to steady her. Faster and faster, they cantered, until he rolled them onto the bed so that Renny was on her back again beneath him. Then he rose to his knees and, gripping her ankles in both hands, spread her wide. With a few more thrusts, he drove himself as deep as he could, then spilled himself inside her until he had nothing left to give. Renny cried out at their culmination, a rocket of heat spiraling through her. She felt as if she would be fused to him forever, hoped they would never be apart again.

And then they were both on their backs, panting for breath and groping for thought, neither seeming to know what the hell had just happened. She gazed up into the candlelit darkness, afraid to look anywhere else. Part of her was already sorry she had succumbed to Tate so quickly, so easily. But part of her couldn't wait for it to happen again.

And that, she supposed, was where the root of her fear lay. That having had Tate once, she would never have him enough. Or, even worse, she would never have him again.

Renny woke to the steady rat-a-tat of rain on the window and smiled sleepily. She loved rain. Rain made the pace of a day seem slower somehow. She always let herself sleep in a few extra minutes when it rained, and she always gave herself a little more time to get ready for work, since no one at Tarrant, Fiver & Twigg ever seemed to be on time, anyway, when it rained. Today would be no exception. Why not relish a few more minutes of semiconsciousness before the day became too full? She sighed with much contentment and reached across the mattress to the nightstand to push the snooze button on her alarm clock...

Only to discover her alarm clock wasn't where it was supposed to be. Nor had it gone off in the first place. When she opened her eyes, she realized her alarm clock wasn't the only thing missing. So was her bedroom. So was her bed. So were her clothes. What the hell? Why was she naked?

She bolted upright at the memories that flooded over her, each more erotic than the one preceding it. Tate unbuttoning her pajama buttons one by one. Tate tracing the lower curve of her breast with his tongue. Tate guiding his fingers between her legs to wreak havoc on the feminine heart of her.

Oh, *that* was why she was naked.

What had she done? Renny Twigg was not the kind of woman who succumbed to a pretty face that easily, that quickly or that passionately. Even faces as pretty as Tate's that were attached to millions— perhaps billions—of dollars. Even in situations of extreme emotional upheaval like the one in which she'd found herself. Her behavior last night had been completely out of character for her.

But maybe, since the situation she and Tate were in was also uncharacteristic, she shouldn't beat herself up for that. No, what she should beat herself up for was not protecting herself by taking proper precautions. She'd told Tate the truth when she assured him the timing wasn't right for her to get pregnant, and she was confident she wouldn't. But the world was full of large families who'd tried to time that sort of thing correctly. And there were other things to worry about with regard to protection—or the lack thereof. Sure, most of them could be addressed with a simple dose of antibiotics, but still.

She had behaved irresponsibly last night. And there was no way she would let that happen again.

So...where did she put her clothes? Or, rather, where had Tate put her clothes? She had a vague memory of her pajama top cartwheeling over her head in a blur of tiny golf carts, but after that, all she could remember was—

Never mind. Best not to think about those things again. She located both the pajama top and bottoms and was knotting the latter at her waist when she registered the aroma of...bacon? Where was that coming from?

She did her best to wind her hair into something that wouldn't lead to the kind of trouble it had led to last night, then tried to look like someone who knew what she was doing as she exited the bedroom. She discovered the answer to the bacon question immediately. Tate was standing in front of the stove—barefoot and shirtless with his jeans dipping low on his hips—stirring something in a frying pan. As she drew nearer, she saw a modest pile of bacon on a plate beside him and what appeared to be scrambled eggs in the pan. There was even something steaming in a saucepan that looked—and kind of smelled—like...the magic bean! Coffee!

For a minute, she thought maybe she was dreaming. That maybe she'd dreamed the entire frenetic night the two of them had shared, because she knew for a fact that there had been no eggs or bacon in the refrigerator the day before, never mind the magic bean. Then she thought maybe Inspector Grady had returned from town with groceries, something that would mean a potential escape from this place, but would also be mortifying for a number of reasons, few of which had anything to do with tiny cartoon golf carts on her person and everything to do with her having woken up naked in someone else's bed.

But no, her dreams had never included smells, so everything, including last night, must be real. Even the part about a gorgeous guy making breakfast in his bare feet.

"Good morning," she said, hoping she injected just the right blend of aplomb and nonchalance into her voice, despite the fact that she felt neither of those things.

When Tate spun around to smile at her, though, he looked as if he felt enough for both of them, something that just made Renny feel even worse. How could he be nonchalant and aplomby about something that had been so passionate and precarious?

"Good morning," he greeted her cheerfully. "You were sleeping so soundly when I woke up, I didn't want to disturb you." He grinned devilishly. "I figured you could use the extra sleep after last night."

Wow, he was really going to go there. And so quickly, too. Renny rushed to change the subject.

Last night was a place she never intended to visit again. Certainly not while the person she'd experienced it with was standing right there in front of her. So she said the only thing she could.

"Coffee. You created coffee. Out of nothing. You must be a god."

He looked a little disappointed that she didn't take his *about last night* comment and run with it. "I kind of created coffee. Out of boiling water. It's instant, so it's more like a coffee impostor. I guess that just makes me a demigod."

Renny didn't care. As long as he poured her some. Which he did. And she tasted it. And it was good.

"Where did you find eggs?" she asked after she'd ingested a few fortifying sips. "I thought Wisconsin was famous for its dairy products, not its roving bands of wild forest chickens."

For a moment, he looked as if he wasn't going to let her get away with changing the subject from what had happened the night before, because he intended to revisit it over and over again. But when he realized she was serious about steering the topic in a new direction, he turned back around to stir the eggs some more.

"They're powdered eggs," he said. "There was a package of them in the cabinet behind the canned stuff. There's some powdered milk up there, too, if you're worried about calcium deficiency."

Oh, sure. What were powdered eggs without pow-dered milk to go with them? From singularly icky to doubly icky. Win-win.

"No, that's okay," she said. "But last time I checked, there was no such thing as powdered bacon. Where did you find that?"

"Freezer," he said, still not looking at her. "One of those foil bricks was what was left of a rasher. No idea how long it's been in there, but it smelled fine."

"It still smells fine," she said. "Thanks for mak-ing breakfast."

He finally looked at her again. He smiled again, too, but the look wasn't quite as cheerful this time. "You're welcome. It's the least I can do for you after last—"

He stopped before finishing, obviously remember-ing her reluctance to talk about what had happened, a surprisingly considerate gesture.

He looked down at the eggs again and repeated softly, "It's the least I can do for you."

So he really was cooking breakfast for her. No guy had ever cooked breakfast for Renny. Even with past boyfriends, when she'd stayed at their place, they always expected her to fix breakfast for them in the morning. It was why she'd always made sure to pick up a bag of doughnuts on her way when she knew she'd be staying over at their places.

"Have a seat," he said. "I'll bring you a plate."

She made her way to the sofa, moving aside the book and magazine she and Tate had discarded there last night before they—

Gah. Was there no escape from thoughts of their lovemaking? Immediately, she corrected herself. They hadn't made love. They'd had sex. A purely physical reaction to a purely physical attraction. Making love was a whole 'nother animal, one she still wasn't sure she'd ever experienced. To make love, you had to be in love. And love was one of those things Renny figured a person didn't know until she felt it. As far as she could tell, she hadn't. Not yet, anyway.

She had just seated herself on the sofa when Tate brought over two plates with identical servings of bacon and eggs. Then he went back for two glasses of orange juice, the concentrate for which, he informed her, had also been lurking under some of the frosted foil in the freezer. A major lover of OJ, Renny enjoyed a healthy taste of it from her glass… only to realize it tasted like freezer-burned aluminum so she immediately spit it back into the vessel again. Much to her horror. The only thing worse than wearing golf-cart pajamas in front of a gorgeous guy was spitting out food in front of a gorgeous guy. Especially food he'd made. But, really, the stuff in that glass… It was way worse than golf-cart pajamas.

Tate looked dashed by her reaction, as if he'd

planted, picked and pressed the fruit in his own backyard, and her rejection of it was tantamount to a rejection of him. "Is there a problem with the juice?" he asked.

"Um, no," Renny lied hastily. Even more hastily, she placed the glass back on the table. "I just remembered, uh…orange juice doesn't agree with me."

Tate didn't look convinced. He picked up his glass, filled his mouth with a hefty quaff…and immediately spit it back out again. "That tastes like the hardware store where my father worked." His gaze flew to hers. "Hey. I remembered something about my father. The store where he worked smelled like metal. Why am I just remembering that?"

Renny smiled back. "I think people's five senses are irrevocably synced with their memory banks. Most of my earliest memories are all of things I could taste or hear or smell."

He nodded, but his thoughts seemed to be a million miles away. Or maybe just a few hundred miles away. In the Indiana town where he'd grown up. Or, rather, where he'd been relocated when he was a toddler.

"Sit. Eat," Renny instructed him gently. "Maybe the bacon will taste like metal, too, and you'll remember even more."

Actually, the bacon tasted like Freon. And the eggs tasted like glue. But Renny managed to consume every bite. Because a gorgeous guy had made breakfast for her and that made everything better.

By the time they finished breakfast, the rain had diminished to a soft patter. So soft that a handful of birds were even singing. Renny went to the window and found that the clouds were less ominous than they'd been the day before. When she opened the window this time, she was greeted by a soft, if still damp, breeze, and that aroma of not-so-far-off water.

She inhaled deeply, relishing the fresh air. She liked living in New York, but some days she needed to be surrounded by green space. As bad as it was to be forcibly separated from civilization, it was kind of nice to be forcibly separated from civilization. And now that the rain was letting up some...

"We should get outside today," she said impulsively.

She turned to find Tate looking at her as if she'd just told him they should fly to Mars.

"What?" he asked.

"We should get out of the cottage for a while," she repeated. "Go exploring."

"Are you nuts? Everything out there is soaking wet."

"Then let's go fishing. If Inspector Grady doesn't make it back today—and considering last night's rain, there's a good chance he won't—then I'll make whatever we catch for dinner tonight. It's the least I can do for the guy who made me breakfast."

She might as well have told him they should drink hemlock for dinner, so repelled did he look by the suggestion.

"Really," she said. "We can't be far from water. It might even be Lake Michigan. Maybe there's a boat or something we could take out."

"You want to fish in Lake Michigan?" he said dubiously. "You want to *eat* the fish you catch in Lake Michigan? Do you know how many industries dump waste into Lake Michigan?"

"We're hundreds of miles away from Chicago. Wisconsin lake water has to be totally different from Chicago lake water."

"Funny thing about water. It does this thing where it moves around a lot. 'Flowing,' I think, is the word they use for it. That means the water—and fish— around Chicago could easily make their way to Wisconsin. Along with all the toxic waste they've consumed beforehand."

"Oh, please. You just ate bacon and eggs that might have been brought here by Donnie Brasco."

"Yeah, but that's a one-off from my usual eating habits. It's not like I eat crap every day."

"At least fish is whole food," she said. "Who knows what goes into powdered eggs? Not eggs, I bet."

He said nothing, but she could tell by his expression that he wasn't going to back down.

"Fine," she relented. "You don't have to eat what we catch. There will just be that much more for me. We're still going fishing. Because if I have to be cooped up in this cottage for another day…"

She let her voice trail off. Not because she figured an unspoken threat was a much more ominous threat, even if that was true. But because she started actually thinking about what would happen if she had to be cooped up in the cottage for another day. And it bore a striking resemblance to what had happened in the cottage last night.

Fishing, she reminded herself. She and Tate would spend the day fishing. Just as soon as she could find something to wear.

Tate had to give Renata credit for one thing. Well, actually, he had to give her credit for a lot of things. But most of those he probably shouldn't mention, since she'd made clear she didn't want to talk about last night. The one thing he could give her credit for at the moment was that she could take a man's gigantic lavender shirt and turn it into…something else. Something without sleeves, since she'd ripped those off and tied them together to make a belt—or something—and with some kind of complicated tying maneuver at the bottom that turned that part of the shirt into shorts that fell just above her knees. Sort of. The rest of the garment was baggy and unhindered by anything resembling a pattern. To him, it just looked like, well…

"It's a romper," she told him in a voice that indicated he should know exactly what that meant.

"So it's for romping?" he asked. "Women have to have special clothes for that?" Frankly, his idea of romping worked a lot better with no clothes at all.

"No, a romper isn't for romping. It's for…" She expelled an irritated sound. "How the hell do I know what a romper is for? Some fashion designer sewed a shirt and shorts together at some point, called it a romper and it stuck. The fashion world hates women, you know. They make us buy things we don't want or need. Hence—" she swept her hands from her shoulders to her knees "—the romper." Now she settled her hands on her hips. "Hey, it beats golf-cart pajamas. Especially for fishing."

Tate battled the urge to shake his head. She really was the strangest woman he'd ever met. Not that he meant that in a disparaging way. Which was weird because, until now, he'd always considered strange people in a disparaging way. Renata brought a certain flair to strangeness. Even her romper had a certain, uh, je ne sais quoi. For lack of a proper industry term. Which probably didn't exist for an outfit like that.

They'd been cleaning up breakfast when Inspector Grady called again to tell them the roads were still out, he was still stuck in Pattypan and it could be another twenty-four hours before he could get to them. But, on the upside, the tech guys were making some headway into the computer breach that had exposed Tate's identity, and with any luck, they'd soon know exactly who John Smith on Craigslist was and just how far his crimes went.

The news that Tate and Renata were going to be stuck here for another day should have been calamitous. Instead, neither of them had been that broken up by it. In fact, it had cemented her conviction that they should spend the day fishing, and she'd gone in search of gear. A closet near the kitchen held a number of discoveries, not the least of which was a stack of board games—something she'd been so excited about she might have stumbled upon the Hope Diamond. Mixed in with them was a quartet of fishing rods and all their accessories.

Satisfied they had all the necessary accoutrements, she'd headed to the bedroom to see what she could do with the remaining clothing. Forty-five minutes later, she emerged in her current getup. He supposed it could sort of qualify for resort wear. In some parts of the world. Where people didn't have any taste.

"What about shoes?" he asked, noting her bare feet. Of course, he was still barefoot, too, but he at least had his polo boots to wear. She only had heels.

"Barefoot is fine," she said. "I love going bare-foot. I never wore shoes when I was a kid. Unless my mom caught me."

Her last statement was short, but she'd delivered it in a tone of voice that spoke volumes. Tate could relate. As much as he'd tried to please his mother and stepfather, he'd never felt he succeeded. Even before that, his mother had always given off a vibe that he was somehow disappointing her. Knowing what he did now, maybe that had had more to do with the fact that his father's family was a little unsavory. Back then, though, he had felt like it was his fault. With his stepfather, he'd always felt like maybe the guy saw him as a reminder that his mother had been involved with another man before him. Or maybe, he, too, thought Tate's origins weren't up to snuff.

Oh, hell, what did it matter? Neither of them was around anymore, and Tate had more than made a success of himself. If parts of his family tree were blighted, that wasn't his fault, was it? You couldn't blame a child for the gene pool that spawned it. Well, you could—and a lot of people did—but it wasn't fair. It wasn't right, either. Lots of people rose above humble, or even lurid, beginnings to make good.

Having obviously given up on his approval of her wardrobe, Renata collected the fishing poles and tackle she'd set aside earlier. "Come on. There's finally a break in the rain. The fish will be looking for food."

"We don't have any bait," he said, making one last-ditch effort to get out of fishing and spend the day in the great indoors instead. Now that the heat had broken—some—it might even be tolerable.

"Fish love freezer-burned bacon. Trust me."

As if he had any choice. He'd never been fishing in his life. She could tell him fish spent their days dancing the merengue in funny hats, and he'd have no way to disprove it.

"Fine," he relented. "But if we haven't caught anything after an hour, we're coming back here."

"Two hours," she bargained.

"Ninety minutes."

She stuck out her hand and smiled. "Deal."

Nine

An hour after slinging their fishing lines into the lake, they'd actually caught three fish, and Tate was itching to catch more. It wasn't Lake Michigan they'd discovered, after all, but Lake Something Else that was small enough to be ensconced by wilderness all around its perimeter. A pier extended a good thirty or forty feet from the shoreline, so they'd made their way to the end of it, sat on its edge and plunked their lines into deep water.

Renata caught the first fish within fifteen minutes of their arrival, a six-inch trout whose breed she'd recognized immediately, and which she'd thrown back in, saying it wasn't big enough. She'd handled it with a confidence he'd envied, then deftly baited the hook again, cast out the line with an easy whir and, after another ten minutes, caught a second, larger trout. Deeming it worthy of dinner, she'd stashed it in the cooler she'd also salvaged from the closet.

It had taken Tate nearly an hour to catch his fish, and it hadn't been much bigger than the first one Renata had caught. She'd been about to throw it back, too, but he rebelled, feeling pretty damned proud of his prize. So she'd smiled like an indulgent scoutmaster and stowed it in the cooler with the first. Then she'd caught the next one. She was two up on him, and hers were bigger. He was competitive enough to find that unacceptable. The next catch would be his, and it would be twice the size of her first one, or his name wasn't Tate Hawthorne. Then again, in reality, his name wasn't Tate Hawthorne, but that was beside the point.

"What's that smile for?"

He looked over to find Renata watching him with laughing eyes. "What smile?" he asked.

"You're grinning like an eight-year-old boy who just caught his first fish," she said.

"That's because I'm a thirty-two-year-old man who just caught my first fish."

She chuckled. "So there's still an eight-year-old boy in there somewhere."

Before today, Tate would have denied that. Hell, he didn't think he'd been an eight-year-old boy even when he was eight. He couldn't remember ever feeling like a child. Whenever he looked back at that time, there seemed to be such a pall over everything. His mother's fear and unhappiness, their struggle just to get through any given day, his small circle of friends that seemed to grow smaller with every passing year.

But he almost felt like a child today, sitting at the edge of a lake pier with his jeans rolled up and his legs dangling above the water. Although the sun was still stuck behind a broad slab of gray, the rain had finally stopped. Birds barnstormed the trees, warbling their happiness at being active again. The wind whispered over their heads, dragging along the scent of pine. Dragonflies darted along the water, leaving trails of what could have been pixie dust in their wakes.

And he'd caught a fish! All in all, not a bad way to spend an afternoon. He wished he'd known a few days like this when he was a kid. Or even one day like this when he was a kid.

He looked at Renata again. She sat on his left, her bare feet hovering within inches of his, her hair half in and half out of a lopsided topknot. Maybe if he'd met a girl like her when he was a boy, he would have had a few days like this one. She looked far more suited to this life—even in her ridiculous romper, which, he had to admit, was less ridiculous than it had seemed a little while ago—than she did to the one that demanded the crisp suit and hairstyle she'd worn when she'd shown up at his front door... Was that only yesterday morning? It felt like a lifetime had passed since then.

"Were you like this when you were a kid?" he asked impulsively.

He had meant for the question to be playful. He had thought it would make her smile. Instead, she sobered.

"Like what?" she asked.

He struggled to find the right words. He'd never been at a loss to describe something, but Renata defied description. "Adventurous," he finally said. Then a few more adjectives popped into his head. "Spontaneous. Unpredictable. Resourceful."

She looked more uncomfortable with every word he spoke. "I don't think I'm any of those things now."

He was about to call her on that—she was all those things and more—but he didn't want to see her withdraw further. Hoping to pull her back from wherever she was retreating, he asked, "Then what were you like as a kid?"

At first he thought she wouldn't answer that question, either. She seemed as determined to ignore it as she was what happened last night. She just reeled in her line until the hook came out of the water empty of even the bacon she had threaded onto it. She looked at the evidence of the one that got away, sighed dispiritedly, then reached into the tackle box for more bait.

And as she went about fixing it on the hook, she said, "As a child, I was…out of place."

He remembered their conversation of the day before, about how she'd attended one of those tony private schools with marble floors and mahogany paneling. He hadn't been surprised by the revelation then. Yesterday, that background had suited her. But looking at her now, he would never peg her as a product of that environment. In his line of work, he knew a lot of people who had grown up that way, clients and colleagues both, and none of them was like Renata. Then again, he wasn't sure if anyone was like Renata. He liked all those other people fine—some he even called friends. But he didn't feel he had a lot in common with them, even living in that world now himself.

He felt he had something in common with Renata, though, despite their disparate beginnings. He wasn't sure what, but they seemed to be kindred spirits. Maybe that was why they'd responded to each other so quickly. He'd been thinking last night was a result of the situation, not the woman. She really wasn't his type. Small, dark and chipper had never turned him on. But Renata did. And now that she did—

Now that she did, she didn't seem inclined to act on the attraction again. Which should have been fine with him. When it came to sex, Tate was pragmatic. Women came and went. He had fun with the ones who wanted to have fun until one or both of them grew tired of it, and then he moved on. Sometimes that happened after months, sometimes it happened after hours. It was looking like Renata was going to be one of those one-timers. So he should be in moving-on mode himself.

Strange thing was, he wasn't ready to move on. He was just starting to get to know her. And he wanted to know more. Those were both new developments. He was never the one who was finished with an encounter last. And he never wanted to know more about a woman than what was on the surface. It wasn't that he was shallow. It was just the way he was. At least, that was what he'd always thought.

It was a big day for firsts. All because of a woman who, twenty-four hours ago, he was wishing had never entered his life.

And he still didn't know what she'd been like when she was a kid. Except for thinking she was out of place.

But instead of asking her to elaborate on what she'd said, he said softly, "Me, too."

Maybe he'd been right about her being adventurous, spontaneous, unpredictable and resourceful as a kid. He could see how all those things would make her feel out of place in a world that valued tradition, orderliness and direction. Funny how he'd yearned for all those things in his childhood, without finding any of them.

They continued to fish in silence for a while, but it wasn't an uncomfortable silence. Nor was it exactly silent silence. The birds and bugs and beasts made sure of that, as did the wind and woods and water. It was almost as if time had dropped them here and stopped, freezing the moment for them because it was so damned near perfect. The only thing that would have made it better was a promise that it would go on forever.

And of all the firsts he'd experienced that day, that one was a monster. He was divorced from every single thing that gave his life meaning—his work, his home, his society, his technology—and there was a not-so-little part of him hoping to stay that way forever. How was that even possible?

He looked at Renata again. She had cast her line back into the water, but she didn't seem to be paying much attention to it. Her gaze was on the opposite shoreline—not that she seemed to be focused on that, either—and her expression was far too somber for someone who should be having fun.

Not sure where the impulse came from, Tate

stretched one leg far enough to dip it into the lake, then kicked hard enough to send a small arc of water splashing over her. She squealed in indignant outrage, looking at him as if she couldn't believe he'd done what he did. He couldn't believe he'd done it, either. He was never this spontaneous or unpredictable. Then she smiled devilishly and dipped her own foot into the water. Or, at least, tried to. Unfortunately, her legs were too short to make it.

So Tate took advantage of her disadvantage and splashed her with his foot again.

"Hey! No fair!" she cried.

He was about to retort that all was fair in love and war, but since this was neither, he supposed she was right. But that didn't mean he had to play by the rules. Even though he'd lived his entire life playing by the rules.

He splashed her again.

She gaped even more incredulously. Then she put down her fishing pole and scooted closer to the edge of the pier, stretching her leg as far as it would go. She managed to get a couple of toes submerged, but when she tried to splash him back, all she achieved was a tiny blip of water that barely broke the surface. Tate laughed and splashed her again.

"Why, you little…" she muttered.

She tried to submerge her foot farther but nearly fell off the pier, righting herself at the last minute.

Tate laughed some more, then watched with much amusement as she maneuvered herself onto her stomach, her arms dangling over the pier.

"Nice try," he said. "Your arms aren't any longer than your legs, small fry."

"Don't you dare call me 'small fry.' Sean Malone used to call me that, and he lived to regret it."

"Who's Sean Malone? Ex-boyfriend?"

Tate was surprised when a thread of jealousy wound through him. What did he care if Sean Malone was one of her ex-boyfriends? What did he care if he was a current boyfriend? He and Renata would never see each other again once this disaster was sorted out. Which felt less like a disaster today than it had yesterday. They'd still never see each other again after it ended. So whoever Sean Malone was, Tate didn't care. Except that he did, kind of.

"Sean Malone was the scourge of fifth grade," Renata said as she wormed her way closer to the edge of the pier again. "He had a nickname for everyone. Mine was 'small fry.' Until the day his locker started reeking with the massive stench of seafood gone bad, and he was sent to the head of school's office, where they put a mark on his permanent record. The entire east wing of Suffolk Academy had to be fumigated."

"And how exactly did the massive stench of seafood gone bad make its way to the entire east wing of Suffolk Academy?"

She grinned with much satisfaction. "It's amazing how bad a ten-piece deep-fried shrimp meal can smell if it's not refrigerated. Especially if you douse it with blue cheese dressing before you stash it in the locker of someone who's a complete slob and would never notice it until it started to reek. It took three days for it to really start stinking up the place, but once it did... Woo. And once Sean realized who was responsible, he never called me 'small fry' again. You, too, will live to regret it."

She stretched her arm as far as she could toward the water, but was still an inch or two shy of reaching it.

"Oh, yeah," Tate said. "I'm shaking in my boots."

He was about to splash her again when, with a final heroic effort, she pushed herself forward, thrust her hand into the lake and hit him with a palm-sized arc of water right in the face. Fortunately, she had small palms. Unfortunately, she also had bad leverage. He opened his eyes just in time to see her go tumbling into the lake headfirst.

She broke the surface immediately, sputtering indignantly, but quickly began to laugh. She pushed a few strands of hair out of her eyes, treaded water and said, "It was worth it to see the look on your face. I guess not too many people try to get even with you for stuff."

Tate grinned as he wiped the last of the water

from his face. "I'm sure a lot of them would like to. They're just too busy."

She paddled back to the pier, and he extended a hand to help her up. She accepted it gratefully...then yanked him into the water alongside her. He had just enough time to suck in a breath before he went under, but when he broke the surface, it was to exhale in a burst of laughter. Renata was cute when she was trying to be vengeful and smug.

They paddled around each other for a moment, each trying to figure out if the other planned further retribution. Then she rolled onto her back to float and closed her eyes. She looked like someone who had all the time in the world to just drift around a Wisconsin lake without a care in the world. So Tate turned his body until he was floating, too. A curious dragonfly buzzed over him for a moment, then darted off. He watched until it disappeared into the trees, then looked up at the clouds. He couldn't remember the last time he'd gone swimming for more than laps at the gym. Hell, he couldn't remember the last time he'd looked up at the clouds. He wondered why not. Then he closed his eyes, too.

"You know," he heard Renata say from what sounded like a very great distance, "Grady could have done a lot worse by us when it came to choosing a safe house."

Her mention of the marshal brought Tate up short.

He had momentarily forgotten why the two of them were here. He'd been having such a good time it felt like they'd planned this excursion months ago and finally found the time to sneak away from their jobs to enjoy it. He'd almost forgotten that, this time yesterday, they were practically strangers.

"On TV," she continued, "the cops always stash protected witnesses in some crappy no-tell motel and make them eat Taco Taberna carryout."

"Yeah, Beefaroni and powdered eggs are so much better," he said wryly.

"Don't be dissing my Beefaroni again, mister."

Tate smiled. "Sorry. My bad."

"I just meant that if we have to be held prisoner somewhere, there are worse places than a Wisconsin wilderness."

Until today, Tate would have said having to live any place whose population fell below two million would be hell. What was life without having everything you wanted at your fingertips? The Big Cheese Motor-Inn didn't even have basic cable. Talk about no-frills living. But he had to admit Renata might be right. Grady could have done worse than lakefronts and dragonflies.

"How much longer do you think we'll be here?"

He was surprised it was Renata asking the question. Then again, she didn't sound like someone who was anxious to leave. She sounded like someone who wanted to stay as long as possible.

"I don't know," he said. Funny, but he kind of sounded like someone who wanted to stay, too. "I guess until the feds locate the person who found me for you and make sure my information didn't go any farther than you."

He heard a splash in the water and opened his eyes. They'd drifted away from the pier, and Renata was swimming back to it. He watched as she gripped the edge with both hands and tried to hoist herself up, but it quickly became clear that she wouldn't be able to manage it on her own. Maybe she didn't like being called a small fry, but...she was a small fry. No shame in that. But there was no way she was getting out of the water on her own, either.

Tate swam to join her and did his best not to make it look effortless when he grabbed the edge of the pier and lifted himself up onto it. She tried valiantly to mirror his actions, but it finally became as clear to her that there was no way she was going to make it. Silently, he dropped to his knees and extended a hand to her again. Even more effortlessly than he had pulled himself out of the water, he tugged her to the pier with him.

And instantly regretted it.

Soaked to the skin as she was, her so-called romper was clinging to every inch of her as if it was skin. And

since she had forgone her still-damp underwear—as
he had himself, something he really didn't need to be
thinking about right now—it left absolutely nothing
to the imagination. Her breasts pushed against the
wet fabric, her quarter-sized areolae pink and perfect, her nipples stiff and tight. He remembered the
feel of them in his mouth, so soft and hot, and it was
all he could do not to duck his head to them again.
Lower, the indentation of her navel beckoned, drawing his eye lower still, to the shadowy triangle at the
apex of her legs. Unable to help himself, he roped an
arm around her waist and covered her mouth with
his, at the same time scooting his other hand down
her torso to dip it between her thighs. She uttered a
single small sound of protest, then melted into him
and kissed him back.

Everything around him dissolved into nothing
after that. All Tate registered was the feel of her
mouth under his and the fabric of her shirt beneath
his fingers. Hastily, he unbuttoned that part of the
garment so he could tuck his hand inside. Then he
furrowed his fingers into her damp flesh, catching
the button of her clitoris between his knuckles before penetrating her with his middle finger. When
she gasped at the invasion, he widened their mouths,
tasting her more deeply. He felt her hand at his waist,
unfastening his jeans, and then she was touching him

just as intimately. Within seconds, he was hard as a rock and ready to rumble.

Where had this come from? This uncontrollable urge to touch her? To have her? He was never like this with other women. He was a disciplined, thorough lover. He liked to take his time. He could keep himself and his partner on a slow simmer until they were both ready to notch it higher. Hell, seduction was half the fun, even when it wasn't necessary because both parties knew they'd be in bed before the night was over.

But with Renata, there was no discipline. There was no simmer. There was just an explosion of wanting and heat and demand. One minute, he was laughing and playful, and the next, he was consumed by a need for her that was so powerful it superseded everything else. They weren't even inside the cabin. They were standing out in the middle of the world where anything could happen, where anyone could see them, even if they were, for the moment, alone. And he didn't even care. Hell, that just made it more exciting.

He withdrew his hand from her shirt long enough to unfasten the rest of the buttons. Then he peeled the wet garment from her body until she stood before him naked. He broke the kiss long enough to strip off his shirt and lower his jeans, and then...

They gazed at each other, silent save for their

panting, her hands on his chest, his on her waist. No way could they make love on the pier—too many splinters. But making love in the water with the fish didn't hold much appeal, either. And there was no way he'd make it back to the motel without going off like a rocket.

He tightened his grip on her waist and lifted her into his arms. Her eyes widened when she realized his intention, but she roped her legs around his waist and her arms around his neck, then held on tight as he lowered her over his raging shaft. He slid into her so easily he might have been a missing part of her. Or maybe she was a missing part of him. He only knew they fitted together perfectly.

He bucked his hips upward as he pushed hers down, then repeated the action in reverse, relishing the hot friction. Something about the angle of their vertical bodies brought a new dimension to the sensation, and he knew he wouldn't last long. Not wanting her to be cheated, he braced one arm tightly around her waist and let the other go exploring, down over the curves of her ass, into the delicate crease that bisected it, pushing the tip of one finger into the dimple he found there.

She cried out again at this new intrusion, so he gave her a moment to adjust. She buried her head in the curve of his neck and shoulder and murmured her approval. So he jerked his hips up again, burying himself completely inside her, and gripped her bottom tighter as he deftly fingered her there.

He held off coming as long as he could, but within minutes, he was surging inside her. She tightened around him and cried out her own completion, bucking against him one final time before going limp in his arms. Carefully, he withdrew from her and lowered her back to the ground. But he didn't—couldn't—let her go. For long moments, they clung to each other, their bodies slick from their swim and the aftermath of their passion. In the distance, thunder rumbled, silencing the chatter of the birds. The water rippled below them, and the wind whispered above them, but Tate was pretty sure its cool caress wasn't why they were both shivering.

Nothing like this had ever happened to him before. And somewhere deep inside, he knew nothing like this would ever happen again. Not the lovemaking in the great outdoors so much, but...something else. Something he wasn't sure he could identify. Something he wasn't sure he *should* identify. Because somehow he knew it had nothing to do with a Wisconsin lakefront.

And everything to do with Renata Twigg.

Ten

By the time Renny and Tate made their way back to the cottage, the sun was beginning its dip toward the trees. In the hours since leaving the motel, they'd put a half-dozen fish in the cooler, filled a T-shirt with wild blackberries, discovered a waterfall, explored a small cave and collected enough pinecones and interesting-looking rocks to fill a pinecone-and-interesting-looking-rocks room in the Smithsonian.

Oh, yeah. And they'd made love in a way Renny would have sworn wasn't possible. Not just the position, but the way it shattered her entire being, too.

She had been totally unprepared for Tate this

afternoon…and yet totally ready for him, too. As quickly and feverishly as things had escalated, as wild and wanton as he'd made her feel, as far as she'd allowed things to go after swearing she would never let them go that far again…somehow it all seemed perfectly in keeping with the way of the world. With the way of Renny. At least the way the world and Renny had been since coming here. Being wild and wanton with Tate just felt right somehow. Being with Tate period felt right. It felt normal. With him, here in this place, she felt more like herself than she ever had with anyone anywhere before. And she felt as if she had been with him, here in this place, forever. It was weird. But nice.

Maybe too nice. She was starting to kind of wish the two of them could stay here like this forever.

Probably best not to think about it. She had dinner to make—she'd promised, since Tate made breakfast. Good thing, too, because he'd told her he'd never cleaned a fish in his life and made clear he had no plans to do it that didn't involve a zombie apocalypse—and even then the whole fish-cleaning thing was iffy, since there would be plenty of grocery stores ripe for the pillaging of peanut butter and jelly.

By the time dinner was on the coffee table—pan-fried trout with a blackberry reduction—the strange heat that had arced between them that afternoon was nearly forgotten. For the most part. Just to be on the safe side, Renny had changed back into her ugly pajamas after her shower when they got back to the cottage—not that those had been much of a deterrent the night before—and Tate was back in his polo jodhpurs and a different white T-shirt. Their clothes from earlier were drying in the bathroom. Not that Renny was in any hurry to put on the alleged romper again. Not without proper underwear next time, anyway. Ahem.

In spite of that, she couldn't quite keep herself from lighting a couple of the emergency candles and setting them on the coffee table with their dinner. Not because it was romantic, but because, um, they provided some nice ambience. Yeah, that was it. The only thing that could have made the setting more romantic…uh, she meant ambient…was if they'd had a bottle of wine to go with their meal. Then again, if previous occupants to the place and their golf-cart pajamas were any indication, it would probably have been a bottle of Wiseguy Vineyards Lambrusco, vintage last week. So maybe it was just as well.

If Tate noticed the romantic…uh, ambient…candles when he sat down, he didn't mention them. She wondered how he felt about what had happened on the pier this afternoon. About what had happened last night. About everything that had happened since the two of them arrived here. Was he as surprised and dazed as she was about their responses to each other?

Did he feel the same sense of timelessness and otherworldliness about the last two days that she did? Or was all of this just an inconvenience and ordeal for him to have to get through, and he was just doing whatever he had to do to stay sane? He had told her sex would be a nice way to pass the time. Was that really all it was to him? Why couldn't that be all it was to her?

And what the hell was she supposed to do about the whole hacking thing? She could end their forced confinement here by admitting to Inspector Grady that she knew perfectly well who had hacked the system and located Tate for her and reveal Phoebe's identity. But that would open Phoebe up to federal charges. And probably Renny, too, for being a part of it. What was weird, though, was that Renny was worried less about federal charges and time in the state pen than about Tate's reaction to her admission that she could have prevented this entire episode— or could end it at any time—by just telling the truth. She didn't want to admit anything, and she didn't want to end it right away. And deep down, that had nothing to do with her fear of federal charges and time in the state pen.

In spite of the jumble of thoughts and questions plaguing her, Renny enjoyed her dinner with Tate. They were so comfortable together at this point that they could have been any normal couple eating in their own dining room, the way they would every night—even though they weren't a couple. Then they cleaned up afterward in the same comfortable way. Once that was done, however, they both seemed to be at loose ends. Neither seemed interested in reading, the way they had done the night before, but neither seemed willing to broach the subject of other pursuits. Probably because the pursuit the two of them had enjoyed together the most since their arrival was sex. So it only made sense for Renny to suggest—

"Scrabble," she said, once the last of the dishes were put away. "We should play Scrabble. Everybody loves Scrabble, right?"

Judging by Tate's expression, he didn't love Scrabble.

Even so, she hurried to the closet and pulled the game out from the middle of a stack of other board games. When she turned back around, Tate was still standing in the kitchenette, looking like he didn't love Scrabble.

"Or there's Trivial Pursuit," she said, thinking maybe he was more of a trivia buff. "Or Monopoly." Which actually might have been the best choice, because that game went on forever and had the most potential to keep them out of trouble.

He shook his head. "Scrabble is fine."

Before he could change his mind, she scrambled to the sofa and opened the board, putting one wooden rack on her side, and the other on his. As she turned the letter tiles upside down in the box lid—the letter bag was missing, as were a number of tiles, she couldn't help noticing—Tate strode to the chair and moved it closer to the table. By the time he sat down, she had mixed up the letter tiles and chosen her seven. All but one were consonants, but the vowel was at least an *A*. Even so, it would probably be best to let Tate go first, so she could play off whatever he spelled.

"You go first," she said magnanimously.

He weighed his options for a moment, sorting his letters into different combinations. Then he used every single letter he had to spell out *P-H-A-R-Y-N-X*, with the *Y* on the double letter square. Not to mention the extra fifty points for using all his letters.

"What?" she cried. "That's one hundred and fifty-two points, right off the bat!" And of course he had positioned the word so that it was impossible for her to make it plural, even if she did manage to pick an *E* and an *S* at some point.

Tate grinned as he collected seven more tiles. "You're the one who wanted to play Scrabble. Everybody loves Scrabble, right?"

Oh, hardy-har-har-har. Fine. She'd show him. At some point. Once she picked an *E* and a *U* to go with her *C*, *F*, *K* and *R*. In the meantime, she used her *A* and *W* with his *P* to spell *P-A-W*. At least that last letter was on a triple letter square. Sixteen points. Not too horribly embarrassing. Except for it being a measly three letters.

"So obviously, you're great at Scrabble," she said. "You must play it a lot."

"Actually, no," he said as he arranged his new tiles. "I like words. I was a huge reader when I was a kid."

She remembered his description of his solitary childhood. Of course he'd been a big reader, if he was alone a lot. But Renny's youthful society had been packed with other kids and tons of activities, and she'd been a big reader, too. All the better to escape that society and those activities, inevitably the kind that had dictated specific roles for male and female alike, and the latter had too often included things like, well, pink tutus.

"What was your favorite book when you were a kid?" she asked.

"Anything with knights and castles. You?"

"Anything with pioneer girls."

He smiled. "Renata Ingalls Wilder."

She smiled back. "Pretty much. Is that why you bought your house? Because it looks like a castle?"

He'd been about to lay down another word but halted. "Noticed that similarity, did you?"

"Kind of impossible not to."

He nodded, then used the *X* he'd used in *P-H-A-R-Y-N-X* to spell out *X-R-A-Y-S*. Dammit.

"The reason I liked castles," he said as he collected four more tiles from the box lid, "was that they're impenetrable. Nobody can get to you when you're in a castle, you know? No Viking hordes in longboats. No lance-bearing Napoleonic armies. No katana-swinging ninjas. No light-saber-wielding Sith lords. Maybe I was trying to find reasons for why I was always alone myself. If I lived in a castle, of course no one would be able to enter my life."

"But you're not alone anymore," she said. A man like him must have scores of friends. "Why do you live in a castle now?"

Still looking at his letters, he replied, "Same reason."

"But—"

"It's your turn," he interrupted her.

Crap. She didn't have any vowels. Hastily, she used her *C*, *R* and *F* with the *T* she'd just drawn to spell *C-R-A-F-T* with the *A* in his *P-H-A-R-Y-N-X*. Better. But her replacement letters were all consonants again. They were definitely going to run out of vowels, unless Tate had just drawn enough to spell *onomatopoeia*. So when he used the *A* in *X-R-A-Y-S* to spell *B-A-R-N*, she knew they were in trouble.

"There," he said. "That word should appeal to

your pioneer girl heart. Why were you a fan of early settlers?"

She much preferred to go back to a discussion of his self-inflicted solitary confinement in his castle— why would a man like him want to keep people at bay?—but the look on his face made clear he was finished talking about it.

So she replied, "Because they were leaving behind society to literally forge their own path in the world. They were going someplace where the rules of culture and civilization as they knew it were changed. Not to mention they spent a lot of time outdoors doing cool pioneer stuff."

Tate chuckled. "Your pioneer girl and my knight boy probably would have gotten along pretty well."

"Only if she could have gotten past his walls. I don't have any vowels," she said before he could reply to her comment. "And we've used up all the ones that are already on the board. I'm going to have to pass."

"I don't have any vowels, either," he said. "Maybe we should just start spelling things phonetically."

Oh, sure. Now he told her. After she'd used up the letters she needed for profanity. Hmm. Even for phonetic spelling, she was at something of a disadvantage. So she used a *J* and an *F* with the *N* in *P-H-A-R-Y-N-X* to spell—

"Jiffin," she said.

He narrowed his eyes at her. "That's not phonetic for anything. There's no such word as *jiffin*."

"Sure there is. It's what you're doing when you smear a certain brand of peanut butter on your bread. You're jiffin' it."

He didn't look anywhere near convinced. But he plucked a few tiles from his rack to use her *J* to spell out *D-J-L-G*.

"What the hell is that?" she asked.

"Dijlig," he said.

"Dijlig," she echoed. "That's ridiculous. At least *jiffin* sounds like it *might* be a real word. *Dijlig* is…" She couldn't finish the sentence. Because *dijlig* didn't sound like anything. "I can barely get my tongue around that."

"It's an arcane sex act that was used by the Etruscans," he told her. With a straight face. Impressive. "Interestingly, it involves the tongue. An Etruscan man would say it when he had his mouth pressed against an Etruscan woman's—"

She held up a hand to stop him. "I get it."

He grinned. "Well, you might. If you ask nicely."

Renny felt heat creeping into her face. Among other body parts. So she quickly drew more tiles—none of them vowels—and, using the *G* he'd just placed on the board, hastily spelled out *K-M-S-G*. She was going to tell him it was a popular Korean side dish—sort of like kimchi, except with less cabbage—but he filled in the definition before she had the chance.

"Oh, *kimsig*. That's another good one from the Etruscans. Even more fun than *dijlig*, actually, because for that position, it's the woman doing it, and she uses *her* mouth and tongue to—"

"Your turn," Renny interrupted him again. Not that she wanted him to take another turn, now that he was completely fixated on the Etruscan equivalent of the *Kama Sutra*, but anything was better than hearing him finish that sentence, because the images exploding in her brain were making her want to leap across the table for a never-ending session of both *dijlig* and *kimsig*. But when he put a *P* in front of the *S* in *X-R-A-Y-S* and she noted he was holding a *Y* in his other hand, she quickly rehearsed all the possible vowel combinations that might result. Passy? Pessy? Pissy? Possy? Pus—

She snapped the board shut with all the tiles still inside. Then she shoved everything into the box, closed it and stood.

"Scrabble is a stupid game," she proclaimed. "And, wow, I'm exhausted. This has been such a full day. I think I'm just going to hit the hay. I could really use a good night's sleep."

And without awaiting a reply, Renny fled to the bedroom, closed the door and locked it behind her— since, knowing Tate, he'd conjure an Etruscan word

that meant *roll in the hay*, too. And he'd be delighted
to tell her—and then show her—exactly which body
parts for that went where.

Tate grinned when he heard the sound of the bedroom door locking behind Renata. Had she done that
because she didn't trust him? Or because she didn't
trust herself? He'd noticed the candles at dinner. And
he'd seen the way she was looking at him as he described for her the finer points of fabricated ancient
sexuality. Or, at least, tried to describe them before
she cut him off. Then again, he was pretty sure she'd
gotten the gist of it both times before ending the
game. Shame, really, since Scrabble was a lot more
fun than he remembered.

She was right, though. It had been a hell of a
day. Even so, he couldn't remember enjoying one
more. Which was weird, because until his predin-
ner shower, he'd spent most of it wet and dirty, doing
things that just made him wetter and dirtier. They'd
actually found a cave and explored it. And a waterfall. Okay, so the waterfall had been only about four
feet tall. It was still his first in-the-flesh waterfall
discovery. Thirty-two years old, world traveled and
experienced to the point of jadedness, and he'd just
seen his first waterfall and explored his first cave.

Two days with Renata Twigg, confined to an area
no bigger than a sleep-away camp, and he was learn-

ing and feeling things about himself he'd never been aware of before. Between this and his newly discovered family ties, it was going to be tough to go back to Chicago and pick up where he'd left off.

Then again, did he really want to pick up where he'd left off? All he'd been doing before Renata came along was working all day, seven days a week, with a break here and there on the weekends to play polo or enjoy the charms of whoever happened to be the femme du jour.

There was a reason for that, though, he reminded himself. His life was the way it was because he worked hard to make it that way. He'd worked hard for years to make it that way. And he *liked* how his life was. Of course he wanted to go back to Chicago and pick up where he left off. Neither his newly discovered East Coast Bacco relations nor his Midwestern adventures with Renata Twigg would change anything. Not unless he wanted something to change. And he didn't. His life in Chicago was near perfect. Why mess with that? Just because he'd spent a day that felt, well, really perfect?

It wasn't real, he reminded himself. The way he and Renata had passed today wasn't the way people normally passed a day. Today was… He sighed as he remembered some of the funner things they'd done. Today was like a snow day from school. One of those happy accidents that seemed magical because it was an unexpected gift of something incredibly special—time.

He shook his head at his own weird thoughts. When had he started to think about this sojourn as an unexpected gift or a happy accident? Only yesterday, it had been the worst possible thing that could have happened. Only yesterday, he'd been blaming Renata for ruining his life. Now today he felt grateful to her for showing him how much fun a break in his routine could be.

Clearly, he needed sleep, too. Maybe Renata had done the right thing, putting a closed and locked door between them for the night. They could both recharge after what had been a tumultuous thirty-six hours and start fresh tomorrow. For all he knew, the spell would be broken by then. There was every chance the two of them would wake up fully reverted to the Manhattan attorney and the Chicago business-man. With any luck, Grady would make it back to the motel with good news and give the all clear so Tate and Renata could return to their normal lives. Maybe the dragonflies and blackberry brambles would re-treat to the backs of their brains, where the two of them could visit from time to time when they had a free moment.

Yeah. That was what they both needed. As much fun as today had been, it was just a little break from reality. If every day was like today, then today wouldn't have been so special.

Tomorrow could be completely different. Everything could go back to normal tomorrow.

Even if nothing was ever the same.

Tate woke on the sofa the next morning to the sound of low thunder. He should have been angered by the sound. More rain meant the road to the motel would be at least another day away from being clear enough for Grady to return.

But hearing thunder and knowing it would rain again today didn't make Tate angry. Instead, all he could think was *There's no school today!* Or if not the actual words, then certainly the childlike feeling of delight that accompanied them. Not just because there was no school—or, rather, no work—today, but because he had another day to play, or something, with his new friend, or something, Renata.

He looked at the bedroom door she had closed and locked the night before. It was still closed. Was it locked? He rolled off the sofa and padded to it, curling his fingers over the knob. It turned easily, and he pushed the door open.

Just for a peek, he told himself. Just to make sure she was okay. Or, you know, actually there and not some fey spirit he'd conjured in a feverish dream. But no, there she was, sound asleep on her side, one hand curled loosely in front of her face, the other stuffed under her pillow. Her coffee-colored hair billowed across the rest of the pillow behind her, save for a single silky strand that streamed down her cheek.

Okay, maybe not just a peek, Tate thought. That strand of hair was bound to become an annoyance that woke her up before she was ready. He'd just move that back to join the rest of the heavy mass so it wouldn't be a nuisance.

As quietly as he could, he tiptoed to the bed and, as deftly as he could, tucked a finger under the wayward tress. He was able to brush it back over the crown of her head without waking her, but wasn't as successful when he drew his hand away. Probably because he also couldn't resist skimming his fingertip along her cheek. He couldn't help it. He wanted to see if her skin was as soft and warm as it looked. And it was. Which was why he skimmed the backs of his knuckles across her cheek, too.

Her eyes fluttered open, looking as soft and warm as the rest of her, and she smiled. "Good morning," she said in the dreamy sort of voice women used when—

Actually, Tate wasn't sure when women used a voice like that, all quiet and husky and full of affection. He'd never been with a woman who responded to him that way—as if there weren't any face she'd rather see first thing in the morning than his. Maybe because he so seldom spent the entire night with a woman, so he rarely saw one wake up. Or maybe because the women with whom he did spend the night didn't want anything more out of it than great sex, so they didn't care whose face they saw first thing, either.

And, hell, he and Renata hadn't even spent the night together this time.

"Good morning," he greeted her back, wondering how his voice could have the same affectionate timbre as hers. He cleared his throat and tried again. "It's raining. Again. Doesn't look like Grady will be making it back today, either."

Instead of looking disappointed, she smiled. "Oh, well. Maybe today we can explore the other side of the lake."

The suggestion should have been as off-putting as fishing had been the day before. Instead, he smiled. "Then we're going to need our strength. I'll start breakfast."

Renata smiled back. "Give me a minute to wake up, and I'll help you make breakfast."

Tate leaned closer and murmured, "Give me more than a minute, and I'll help you wake up."

In response, she curled her arm around his neck and pulled him the rest of the way down to kiss him. Their lovemaking this time was slower and more thorough, as if each felt they had all the time in the world to give it. This morning, it did feel like they had all the time in the world. It was a feeling Tate had never experienced—as if he had no obligations, no responsibilities, no plans. He had only Renata. She had only him. At least for today. And tomorrow…

He'd think about tomorrow tomorrow. Today just had too much going for it, jam-packed as it was with dragonflies and waterfalls and Renata.

Eleven

It was a pattern Renny and Tate repeated for the nearly three days that followed. Wake up together, make love together, fix breakfast together. Get a call from Inspector Grady telling them the same thing—that the road to the hotel was still impassable, and the tech guys were still working on the breach. Then go exploring in the rain together, eat dinner together and play Erotic Scrabble together—or Porno Pictionary or Lascivious Pursuit—then shower together, go to bed together, make love together, sleep together and start all over again.

They were insatiable. Not just for each other, but

for everything around them. Over the course of those days, the Wisconsin wilderness became less wild and more welcoming, and adversity became adventure. In a lot of ways, Renny felt more at home here with Tate than she'd ever felt back home with people she'd known her entire life. She'd always loved the great outdoors. As a girl, she'd never seen a tree she didn't climb, never met a bug she didn't befriend, never encountered a puddle she didn't jump in, never passed a rock she didn't pocket. This place was Utopia for a girl like that, and being here brought the girl right back to the surface. Except that here, that girl was allowed to run free.

And, as a woman, she'd never known a man like Tate. One who saw her and knew her the way she really was—the way she really wanted to be—and seemed to like her anyway.

No. Not seemed to. He did like her. There was no way he could respond to her the way he did if he didn't. They talked constantly, about anything and everything. They had fun. They laughed. A lot. And the night the rain clouds finally cleared, they skinny-dipped in the lake, then lay on a blanket on the pier and gazed at millions—perhaps billions—of stars, talking about nothing and everything and being the way they wanted and needed to be. Renny never wanted it to end.

But it did the morning she awoke to the crunch of

gravel outside the bedroom window. Inspector Grady had finally managed to make it back up to the motel.

"Dammit, Tate, wake up," she said urgently as she rolled out of bed. "Grady is back."

Tate mumbled something incoherent as she grabbed her discarded pajamas from the floor. Then he rolled to his side and fell back asleep. She hopped on one foot, then the other, as she yanked on her pajamas and called out to him again, louder this time.

"Tate! Wake up! You have to move to the sofa! Grady is outside!"

As she thrust her arms through the shirtsleeves, she heard the bang of a car door slamming. Tate slept blissfully on.

"Tate!" she tried one last time. He didn't budge.

Fine. Let him look like a jerk, taking the bed and leaving Renny to sleep on the sofa. No way was she going to let Grady know they'd been sharing a bed—and a lake pier and a shower and a sofa and the rug in front of the fireplace—while he was gone. No way was she going to let the marshal find out what had happened during the time she and Tate were here. Not that she was sure herself what had happened. There would be time to think about that later, when she and Tate were home.

Hundreds of miles away from each other.

She let that sink in for a second—how could she and Tate live hundreds of miles away from each other when it felt as if they'd been sharing the same piece of air for a lifetime? Then she grabbed a sheet from the bed, fled the room and closed the door behind her. She had just enough time to lie down on the sofa when the front door opened and Grady announced his arrival. She used it as an excuse to pretend the noise had woken her up, rolling over to greet him in what she hoped was a convincingly slumberous fashion, even though adrenaline was pumping through her body at a rate that would have won her Olympic gold.

"Oh, hi," she said, hopefully in a slumberous manner.

She tried to rouse a yawn, couldn't find one, so opened her mouth and covered it with her hand for a few seconds. In spite of her Olympic prospects at the moment, judging by Grady's expression, she wasn't in the running for an Oscar.

"Sorry to wake you, Ms. Twigg," he said blandly—though, she had to admit, he wasn't exactly in the running for an Oscar, either, since it was clear he wasn't fooled by her sudden wakefulness. "Guess I should have called to let you know I was coming, but I still wasn't sure I'd make it up the hill and didn't want to get your hopes up. Plus, I figured you and Mr. Hawthorne could use the extra sleep."

Gee, why would he assume she and Tate needed the extra sleep?

Probably best not to think about it.

"Well, thank you for your consideration," she said. There was no reason she couldn't be just as vague as Grady.

The bedroom door flew open suddenly, and Tate appeared in the doorway wearing nothing but his borrowed blue jeans, holding his T-shirt in his hand. He looked gorgeous and virile and—there was no way to get around it—recently tumbled, and he did nothing to promote the fallacy Renny was trying so hard to cling to.

"I smell coffee," he said.

Well, good morning to you, too, she wanted to tell him. Of course, her own greeting of *Dammit, Tate* a few minutes ago hadn't exactly been romantic, either, had it? Besides, she didn't want him to be romantic. She didn't. She wanted Grady to think nothing between her and Tate had changed since the last time the marshal had been here. Even though everything had.

"Real coffee," Tate elaborated. Still not being in any way romantic. So, yay, Tate. "Good coffee. Not the powdered horror in a jar we've been having to drink every morning."

Only then did Renny notice that Grady was holding a cardboard drink carrier that housed four cups of covered coffee. When Tate noted the number of cups, his expression turned sublime. "And you brought automatic refills." He jerked on his T-shirt, strode across the room, took the carrier from Grady and marched it to the coffee table, then uncapped one and moved it under his nose for a healthy inhalation. "Oh, baby, baby, come to Daddy."

Renny battled a twinge of jealousy that he was more in love with coffee at the moment than he was with her. Not that she expected him to be in love with her. But he could at least seem happier to see her this morning than he was caffeine.

On the upside, Grady looked a lot more convinced that her having woken up on the sofa was a credible prospect. He looked even more convinced when it became clear Tate had no intention of opening a cup of coffee for Renny. Yay again. Dammit. So she reached for one herself. There was even real cream and sugar to go with it. She couldn't remember the last time she'd had real coffee with real cream and sugar.

Oh, wait. Yes, she could. It had been less than a week ago. Saturday morning, at O'Hare. Why did it keep feeling like years had passed since her arrival in this part of the country?

Tate continued to sip his coffee in silence, so Renny did, too. Grady set a bag on the table decorated with a logo from a place called Debbie Does Donuts, and informed them that the lemon chiffon crullers were particularly good, but not to rule out the maple bacon, because he couldn't believe how well that combination worked in a doughnut. Renny peeked into the bag and snagged a basic glazed. She wasn't feeling especially adventurous this morning.

"I've got good news and bad news," Grady said, when it became clear that neither she nor Tate would be especially talkative. "Which do you want first?"

Still looking at his coffee instead of at Renny, Tate said, "Good."

"Okay. I've been given the official all clear that there's no threat to you, Mr. Hawthorne, and you're free to go."

Tate snapped his head up to meet Grady's gaze. "Just like that?"

The marshal nodded. "You'll be home in a matter of hours. I'll drive you myself."

"Then what's the bad news?"

Grady looked at Renny. "The bad news is for Ms. Twigg."

Something cold and unpleasant settled in her midsection. All she could manage by way of a response was "Oh?"

Grady smiled, but there wasn't an ounce of happiness in the look. "Yeah, oh. Do you want to tell Mr. Hawthorne, Ms. Twigg, or should I?"

That, finally, made Tate look at her. He was clearly confused. For a moment, she could almost convince herself there was no way Grady's techs could have discovered what they had obviously discovered, since she and Tate were being given the all clear. For a moment, she could almost convince herself that the fantasy life they had been enjoying for the last five days really would go on forever.

Even though it was pretty clear Grady had discovered where the security breach originated, Renny told herself to keep her mouth shut. She was an attorney, for God's sake. Maybe she only practiced probate law, but she knew better than to say anything to a law enforcement officer that could be used against her in court. She had Phoebe to think about, too.

When Grady realized Renny wasn't going to be more forthcoming, he said, "Does the name Phoebe Resnick ring a bell, Ms. Twigg?"

Okay, it was *very* clear Grady had discovered where the security breach originated. Even so, Renny still said nothing.

"Who's Phoebe Resnick?" Tate asked, sounding even more confused.

"Also known as the Tandem Menace," Grady told him.

Yep, they knew all about Phoebe. She'd been using that nickname since sixth grade. That was when she discovered a way to get into the school's computer so it looked like the hack was coming from two places at once, only she was really coming in from a third place that didn't show up at all. No one in the administration ever figured out who was doing it or how, and Phoebe went to MIT on full scholarship.

These days, she owned a digital security company that was making her a boatload of money. She still hacked on her days off, but she used her powers only for good. She did things like move money from the accounts of despots into the accounts of human rights organizations. Or she took money from human traffickers and donated it to women's shelters and scholarship funds. Or she transferred money from the accounts of corporations that tested on animals and gave it to the ASPCA. And when a friend needed her, she did things like locate a little boy who'd been buried in a federal database.

"What the hell is a tandem menace?" Tate asked.

Grady continued to look at Renny, offering her the opportunity to clear the air with her own explanation instead of clouding it with an indictment of his own. But if the marshals had IDed Phoebe, they must know Renny was involved, too. Although she and Phoebe had only talked about Tate in person—Phoebe never left a digital trail…um, except this time, evidently—the two of them had been friends since preschool. There was no way Renny could credibly deny her involvement with the hack. And now Tate was going to—

She really didn't want to think about what Tate

was going to do once he learned the whole truth. Which was another reason she didn't say a word.

Grady, however, still had plenty to say. "Phoebe Resnick is a world-class hacker who goes by the moniker the Tandem Menace on the dark web. She's the one who ransacked the WITSEC databases until she located you, Mr. Hawthorne. And, oh, yeah, she's been a friend of Ms. Twigg's since they were kids."

Renny braved a glance at Tate. He still looked confused.

"But you said it was a guy you found on Craigslist named John Smith."

Renny wanted to tell him she never would have trusted his identity to a guy on Craigslist named John Smith and at least be honest about that. But she couldn't even tell him that much. Not with Grady standing there, listening. She felt horrible now for what she had kept hidden from Tate. If she had just been honest that morning in his office when Grady first arrived…

But if she'd done that, she never would have had the last five days with Tate. And the thought of that was even more horrible. Even if she never had another day with him again—and it was more than likely that, after this, she wouldn't—there was a part of Renny that would never be able to regret her transgression.

As the truth finally sank in, Tate gazed at her incredulously. "Your *friend* was the security breach at the Justice Department?"

Renny still said nothing. She couldn't. Although this time it had nothing to do with incriminating herself or Phoebe. This time, it was because Tate was looking at her as if she were the most heinous villain in the world.

"You've known all along there was no threat to my safety?" he asked.

His anger was almost palpable. Renny remained silent.

But Tate wasn't. "This whole fiasco could have been avoided if you'd told Grady on Saturday that you knew who was behind the breach?"

He thought this had been a whole fiasco? Had there been nothing about this week he could think of that made it only a partial fiasco? Like maybe how much fun the two of them had had before all hell broke loose? Like maybe how they'd learned about each other and themselves? Or how they'd come to feel about each other? Or how happy they'd been, if only for a little while?

Tate stood and moved to the other side of the room, though whether that was because he suddenly felt restless, or because he wanted to put as much distance between himself and Renny as possible, she couldn't have said. That became clearer, however, as he spoke further.

"Five days," he said. "Five days we've been stuck here. Five days I've been away from work. Do you know how much I missed being away from work for five days? Do you know how much it cost me to be away from work for five days?"

Renny figured she could answer that, at least, without incriminating herself. Even so, all she could do was shake her head.

"Millions, Renata. It's cost me millions. Worse than that, it's cost my clients millions. It's hurt my business. It's compromised my reputation. It's—"

He stopped pacing, hooked his hands on his hips and glared at her. Then he shook his head and began to pace again. When it became clear that the rest of his tirade would be taking place in his head—which was somehow worse than having him sling it at Renny, because she had no way to defend herself even if her actions were indefensible—she looked at Grady again.

She wanted to ask him what was going to happen to Phoebe, wanted to tell him her friend shouldn't be held responsible for any of it, since Renny was the one who put it all in motion. But she knew the law didn't work like that. The law dealt with actions, not intentions. Phoebe had broken the law. Renny was an accessory. Even if neither of them had meant any harm, they could both be looking at some hefty repercussions. And Phoebe, unfortunately, would bear the brunt of it.

Grady crossed his arms over his chest and studied Renny in silence long enough for her to mentally fit herself and Phoebe for orange jumpsuits and realize that no, orange wasn't actually the new black.

He must have realized what she was thinking, though, because he told her, "Relax, Ms. Twigg. Phoebe made a deal with us. She's going to do some favors for Uncle Sam. In exchange, Uncle Sam is going to look the other way with regard to this one... episode...and pretend it never happened. And since this...episode...never happened," Grady added, "then you couldn't be part of it, could you?"

Renny nodded. "Thanks," she said wearily.

"For what?" Grady asked.

No sense pushing it. Especially since she had a lot more to worry about where Tate was concerned. He was still glaring at her with clear disbelief and even clearer fury. She rose from the sofa to approach him, but he held up a hand to stop her.

"Don't say anything," he told her.

"I can explain," she said halfheartedly.

"I don't want to hear it."

"Tate—" she tried again.

But he turned to Grady and said, "When can we leave?"

"As soon as you're ready," the marshal said. Almost as an afterthought, he looked at Renny. "You, too, Ms. Twigg. I've arranged for a flight for you out of Green Bay, so we'll make a brief stop there on the way to Chicago. I have the belongings you left at Mr. Hawthorne's house in the SUV." He turned back to Tate. "Mr. Hawthorne, please accept my apology on behalf of the United States government for your inconvenience and discomfort this week. We only wanted to ensure that you were protected, as we promised you would be when you entered the program thirty years ago."

"Apology accepted," Tate replied automatically.

Oh, sure. He'd accept an apology from Grady, but he wouldn't even let Renny voice one. Then again, Grady hadn't actually been the person who'd caused Tate inconvenience and discomfort this week, had he? No, all of that fell to Renny. She didn't blame him for being angry at her. She was angry at herself. But she wished he would at least give her a chance to explain.

And she hoped that, someday, on some level, Tate would be able to think about the last five days as having been more than inconvenience and discomfort. She hoped that, someday, he remembered too the blackberry brambles and the pine cones and the star-studded night sky and her.

"I should shower and change," she said quietly. "I'll be as fast as I can."

Before either man could reply, she retreated to the bedroom. As she grabbed her wrinkled suit and blouse from the closet, she tried not to notice Tate's polo uniform hanging beside it and how different the two outfits were from each other. How they didn't belong together at all. How, in normal circumstances, they would never have shared the same space.

And how, now that Renny had ruined everything, they would never share the same space again.

Home, sweet castle.

After almost a week away from it, Tate opened the portcullis, strode through the barbican and surveyed his realm. It seemed a lot smaller than he remembered. And it was so empty. Even Madison wasn't around. Tate had instructed Grady to call the butler and tell him to take time off with pay until Tate returned home. Home to his castle-slash-house that he'd bought because he would be living in a fortress where no one would be able to get to him. For years, no one had.

Not until Renata Twigg.

She changed his life when she showed up with her files and photos. Not just because of what he learned about himself from those files but what he learned about himself in the days that followed, too.

He reminded himself that she hadn't just changed his life—she'd messed it up in a way that would take a long time to fix. Then again, was it really *his* life she'd messed up? Just who was Tate Hawthorne, anyway? The grandson of a reputed New York mobster? A successful Chicago businessman? A babe in the Wisconsin woods? All of the above? None of the above? This week had left his head so full of weirdness he wasn't sure he'd ever know himself again. Not that he'd really known himself before Renata.

Just what the hell had happened to him this week?

He took the stairs two at a time, trying not to notice how the echo of his boots made the house sound—and feel—even emptier. Once in his bedroom, he stripped off the fetid polo uniform and headed for the shower. The massive marble shower with its three jets and bench for two that would have given him and Renata a lot more room to move around than the tiny stall at the motel. In a shower like this, he and Renata could—

Nothing, he told himself. He'd never see her again. She'd lied to him. She'd completely disrupted his life. She'd cost him and his clients a massive amount of money. The last five days had been a total disaster.

Okay, maybe not a total disaster, he backpedaled as he stepped under the jets. But he was happy to be home. He couldn't wait to get back to his normal life. Really. He couldn't. His normal life that would be completely lacking in discomfort and inconvenience and Renata Twigg.

Work, he told himself. He'd been too long away from the thing that gave his life meaning. No wonder he felt so weird. Working grounded him and reminded him what was really important. He needed to work.

He made his way back down the stairs—damn, the house really was way too quiet, even though this must have been the way it always sounded and felt—and made his way to his office. He had a mountain of email waiting, and at least half of them were decorated with the little red exclamation mark that deemed them Important.

But none of the Important emails he read seemed all that important.

Oh, well. He still needed to get back to work. The thing he knew best. The thing he did best. People would come and go in his life. Events would begin and end. But work... That was a constant.

Thankfully, he had enough of it to keep him from thinking about Renata and the damage she'd caused. Enough to keep him from remembering dragonflies and fireflies and picking blackberries with Renata. Enough to forget about counting stars and catching fish and playing Strip Monopoly with Renata. Oh, yeah. He was very, very thankful for all this work.

He went back to the first Important email he'd opened—even if it wasn't all that important—and hit Reply.

* * *

It was raining in New York City. Possibly the same rain that had fallen in Wisconsin earlier in the week. Renny—freshly showered and wearing silk pj's that were blissfully devoid of golf carts—gazed out her living room window at the snaking traffic of Tribeca and told herself again how happy she was to be home.

No more freezer-burned food or homemade rompers. She could binge-watch all the BBC mysteries she wanted and soak in her tub for hours. She could be with people who appreciated her for more than her ability to give them an orgasm and didn't hate her guts. She was elated to be here and not in Wisconsin. She was. Even if there was a part of her that would be in Wisconsin forever.

It was just too bad that part would be there alone.

Tate had been silent on the drive from the motel, and he'd ignored her when she climbed out of the SUV at the airport in Green Bay. Not that she blamed him. But she wished he would have at least said goodbye.

In the days that followed, Renny went about her job robotically, telling herself the reason she was so unenthusiastic about her cases was because she was just having trouble getting back in the groove.

But as the days became weeks, and her groove never materialized, she began to think a little differently. Like how maybe the reason she was the only person at Tarrant, Fiver & Twigg who hadn't always found the heir she was looking for, and the reason she'd screwed up her assignment with Tate, and the reason even the cases she didn't screw up never went as smoothly for her as they did for everyone else, the reason for all those things was because, well, Renny wasn't very good at her job. And the reason she wasn't very good at her job was because she didn't actually like her job. Not the way she should like it. Not the way everyone else at Tarrant, Fiver & Twigg liked theirs.

But after a few weeks back at work, Renny did start to think about that. Not just because of her epiphany that she might not be suited to be a suit at Tarrant, Fiver & Twigg, but because, for the first time since she was twelve years old, she was late. Not late for work. Not late for Zumba. Not late for lunch with friends. Renny was late as in *holy-crap-I-have-to-buy-a-home-pregnancy-test-my-God-how-did-this-happen* late.

Not that she couldn't guess how it happened. Although she'd been confident she was right when she told Tate that first time that the timing was wrong for her to get pregnant, after five days together, the timing might have been just right. So she shouldn't have been surprised one evening to find herself popping into a Duane Reade that was a few—or seventeen—blocks from her condo for some toothpaste, a bottle of biotin, a pack of AAA batteries, the latest issue of *Vanity Fair*, a six pack of Kit Kats and, oh, what the hey, a pregnancy test.

Twenty minutes after she got home, Renny was thinking she might have been better served to pick up a copy of *Parenting* instead of the *Vanity Fair*. But thank God for the Kit Kats. And once that realization set in, another quickly followed it.

HolycrapmyGodhowdidthishappen?

But she already knew how it had happened. So, really, the question she needed to be asking herself was what she was going to do. There was another human being growing inside her that was half Renny and half Tate. Knowing what she did of him, she was sure he would offer financial support. But personal support? That was a tough call. Not only was there the whole hating-her-guts thing to consider, but by now he was back to his usual routine with a work life that included weekend hours and a home office, and a social life that included leggy redheads and evenings out. Would he want any of that interrupted by the patter of little feet and a woman he didn't like? Doubtful.

More to the point, did Renny want her life interrupted? Then again, was her life what and where she wanted it to be in the first place? Not really.

She looked at the little plastic wand in her hand, with its little pink plus sign. And she wondered again what the hell she was going to do.

Twelve

A month after returning from Wisconsin, Tate's life had totally returned to normal. He was back to his normal seven-day workweek, his normal Saturday polo game, his normal Tuesday drinks with friends-slash-colleagues, who, okay, now felt a bit less like friends than they did colleagues. He was also back to his normal nights out with normal leggy redheads— though, admittedly, those nights were slightly less normal, because they always ended early for some reason and never reached their obvious conclusion. Still, except for those small factors, a month after returning from Wisconsin, his life had returned to normal. Totally, totally normal.

Except for how he had never felt less normal in his life.

Almost nothing about his daily existence had changed after that brief hiccup that was five days in Wisconsin. Yet somehow everything about his daily existence felt changed.

He told himself it was because part of his life was still unsettled, since he hadn't been in contact with any of his newly discovered relatives on the East Coast. Tate's attorneys had worked with Tarrant, Fiver & Twigg to complete the paperwork necessary for him to decline his inheritance from Joseph Bacco without revealing his new identity to the rest of the family. He'd been surprised when his attorneys had informed him that his aunts and uncles and cousins wanted to meet him if he was amenable. To the Baccos, family was family, and Joey the Knife had spent thirty years wanting to bring his little grandson back into the fold. Even if Tate didn't want to join the family business, they said, they hoped he would someday see clear to join the family. When he was ready to make himself known to them, they were ready to embrace him with a big ol' Bacco hug. Tate just didn't know yet how he felt about all that.

Deep down, though, he knew it wasn't his uncertainty about his East Coast relations that was the source of his current unrest. Mostly because, deep down, he kind of knew what was the source of that.

The same thing that had been the source of it a month ago. Renata Twigg.

He hadn't heard a word from her since Grady dropped her at the curb—literally—in Green Bay. Once, about a week ago, when he was up late and after a couple of bourbons, he'd Google-imaged "Renata Twigg." But when a dozen photos of her appeared on his computer screen, he spared barely a minute to look at them. Because he was suddenly sleepy enough to go back to bed, not because one of the photos was of her at some society function, looking breathtaking in a black strapless dress, with some upright, forthright, do-right kind of guy on her arm. Even if the photo had been two years old, it was just a reminder that things between them hadn't ended well. More to the point, things between them had ended. She had a life of her own half a continent away that she'd gone back to, and it doubtless had returned to normal, as well. Anyway, there was no reason for him to be Google-imaging her late at night with a couple of bourbons in him.

The next day, he'd called an event planner he knew and hired her to organize an obscenely gigantic party for him, and money was no object if she could get the damned thing put together by the following weekend, because, man, it had just been too long since he'd had an obscenely gigantic party. Which was how Tate came to be hosting a bash for a hundred of his closest friends, right this very minute, in the house-slash-castle he'd bought to keep people out, and which had been way too empty, and way too quiet for, oh, about a month now.

So why wasn't he downstairs having a blast with his hundred closest friends? Why was he, instead, standing on the balcony off his bedroom gazing down at the ones who were prowling around the grounds? Sure, he'd been a good host at first. He'd dressed the part in his best charcoal trousers and a gray linen shirt. He'd greeted everyone at the door and directed them to the three different bars and let them know the DJ would be starting his first set at eight. And he'd made one perfunctory circuit of the goings-on to be sure the noise level was loud enough to indicate everyone was having a good time—it was, and they were. Then he'd fetched a drink from the nearest bar to wait for the spirit of the gathering to overtake him, too.

He was still waiting.

He was about to return to his bedroom when a single guest caught his attention in the garden below. She was standing alone at its very edge, as far removed from the crowd as she could be without actually disappearing. She wore a plain sleeveless dress the color of a Wisconsin wilderness, and her dark hair was shorter than the last time he saw her, just barely brushing her shoulders. He couldn't imagine what had brought Renata to his house—unless it was his thinking about her—but she didn't look happy to be here. In fact, after a sweeping glance at the crowd, she turned around as if she was going to leave.

The music was too loud for her to hear him if he called out to her, so he ran from the bedroom, nearly stumbled down the stairs, raced through the front door and rounded the house on the side where he'd seen her. Thankfully, she'd gotten only as far as the garden boundary nearest him, so he hurried forward to stop her before she could get away. She was looking at the ground, though, so she didn't see him coming, and when she suddenly began to jog away from the goings-on and toward him, he didn't have a chance to move out of her way, and she jogged right into him.

He was able to catch her by the upper arms before she would have bounced backward, but the minute he touched her, all he wanted to do was pull her forward. How had he gone a month without touching her, when he'd touched her every day for—

Five days. Had they really only spent five days together? How was that possible? It felt as if Renata had been a part of him forever. And why, suddenly, was he thinking about all the moments of those days instead of the end of them when he accused her of messing up his life irrevocably? She hadn't messed up his life, he thought now. He'd only thought she messed up his life because she messed up his work, and back then—a whole month ago—work had been his life. But after those five days in Wisconsin with Renata…

Hell, she hadn't messed up his life. She'd saved it.

"Hey," he said softly as he pulled her up, "slow down. Where's the fire?" Other than in his chest, he meant. Because there was a warmth kindling there that was fast spreading.

He thought she would smile at the question, but when she looked up, her mouth was flat, and her eyebrows were knit downward.

"What, you came all this way just to glare at me?" he asked, injecting a lightness into his voice he wasn't close to feeling.

She shook her head. "No. Why I came isn't important now." She hesitated, then stepped backward, out of his grasp. "I have to go."

Before he could object—hell, before he even knew what she was talking about—she hurried past him, heading toward the front of the house. She was doing more than jogging now. She was running. Why had she come all the way to Chicago if she was just going to run away from him? Why hadn't she told him she was coming in the first place? What the hell was going on?

"Renata, wait!" he called after her. But she only ran faster.

So Tate ran after her.

He caught up with her as she was key-fobbing a sedan that was nondescript enough to indicate it was a rental. She had opened the driver's-side door and tossed her purse into the passenger seat when he caught her by the upper arm again. Only this time he did pull her toward him. Before she could stop him— and because he couldn't help himself—he lowered his head to hers and kissed her.

She kissed him back immediately, her body fairly melting into his. Just like that, a month faded away, and the world dissolved around them. All Tate knew was that he had Renata back, and for the first time in weeks, he didn't feel as if he were in the wrong place and time. For the first time in weeks, he felt as if he were exactly where he belonged.

Reluctantly, he ended the kiss. But he didn't go far. He looped his arms around her waist and bent to touch his forehead to hers. He'd forgotten how small she was. Funny how he'd always avoided small women because he thought he wouldn't know what to do with one. He and this one fitted together perfectly. Then again, that didn't have anything to do with their sizes.

"You don't hate me?" she said by way of a greeting.

"I never hated you," he assured her.

She hesitated, gazing into his eyes as if trying to

see the thoughts inside his head. Finally, she said, "That makes one of us. I hate myself for not telling you the truth right away, Tate. I'm sorry for what happened. I'm sorry I wasn't honest with you. I couldn't be. If I'd said anything in front of Grady, it could have put Phoebe in jail for a long time. But I am so sorry I—"

"I'm not sorry for any of it," he said.

For the first time, he realized that was true. Yes, Renata had lied to him. Yes, for five days, his life had been completely disrupted. If she had been honest the first day, none of that would have been the case. But those five days had ended up being the best five days Tate had ever known. In those five days, he had learned more about himself than he had in the thirty-plus years that preceded them. He'd been able to be himself in Wisconsin. He'd discovered himself there. Even more important, he'd discovered Renata. And he'd realized just how much he needed someone like her in his life to make him happy. Really, honestly, genuinely *happy*, something he had never been before.

No, he didn't need someone like Renata for that. He needed Renata.

She looked confused. "But that last day in Wisconsin—"

"That last day in Wisconsin, I didn't realize a lot of things I should have realized that first day in Wisconsin. Like how much I needed five days in Wisconsin. Especially with someone like you. Let's try this again," he said softly. "Hi."

She still looked confused. But she replied, even more softly, "Hi."

"It's good to see you."

"It's good to see you, too."

"I've missed you," he said, surprised not only to realize the feeling, but to reveal it. Not just because he'd never told a woman—or anyone—that he'd missed her before. But because he'd never actually missed a woman—or anyone—before. He'd missed Renata, though. He'd missed her a lot.

"I've missed you, too," she said.

By now her voice had softened so much he barely heard what she said. He felt it, though. He felt it in the way she'd curled the fingers of one hand into his shirt and cupped the other around his neck. And he felt it in the way she nestled her head against his chest. Mostly, though, he felt it in the air around them. As if whatever it was that made them who they were somehow mingled and joined the same way their bodies had so many times before, and now it was finding its missing pieces, too.

For a moment, they only stood entwined, refamiliarizing themselves with all the nuances of each other's bodies and spirits, remembering how it had felt to be so close, enjoying that nearness again.

Tate figured he should wait for Renata to say something first, since she was the one who had traveled across half the country to get here. But she didn't say anything. She just leaned into him as if she never wanted to let him go.

So Tate started instead. "Not that I'm complaining or anything, but what are you doing here?"

She stayed silent for another moment, and he began to think she wouldn't say another word. He even tightened his hold on her a little because he feared she might try to bolt again. But she didn't do that, either. The night closed in around them, the lights of the house and grounds not quite reaching this far, the music of the party a faint burr against the darkness. There was a part of him that would have been perfectly content to stay this way forever. Finally, though, Renata lifted her head from his chest and looked up at him. She still didn't look happy. But she didn't look quite as hurt as she had at first, either.

"I need to tell you something," she said.

He couldn't imagine what. And, truth be told, he wasn't sure he cared. All he knew was that he was with Renata, and the life that had felt so abnormal for the past month suddenly felt right again.

"Okay," he said. "What?"

She freed her fingers from his shirt and dropped her hand from his neck to her side. Then she took a small step backward. But she stopped when he wove his fingers together at the small of her back to keep her from retreating farther. Her reaction wasn't exactly what he had expected. Why had she come this far only to pull away from him? Especially after he'd made clear he wanted her here.

"We need to talk," she said, not telling him what she needed to tell him.

The heat in his midsection took on a new dimension. "I thought that was what we were doing," he said, forcing a smile.

She didn't smile back. She turned to look over her shoulder at his house and the party in full swing inside and behind it. When she looked at him again, the hurt in her expression had returned.

"I should come back tomorrow," she said. "You're entertaining. It's obviously not a good time."

Was she crazy? Not a good time? Didn't she realize the minute he saw her, it was the first good time he'd had in a month?

"Renata, what's going on?" He didn't bother trying to mask his worry now.

"Seriously, it's late," she said. "I don't know what I was thinking to come here this time of night. Well, except maybe that it took me all day to gather my courage. Tomorrow would be better. I'll come back then. What time is good for you?"

She'd been here all day and was just now showing up at his door? She'd had to gather her courage to do that?

"It's barely ten thirty," he said. "That's not late. Especially on a Saturday night."

Her expression changed again, and he could tell she was weighing something very important in her head. He couldn't imagine what would be warring in there to cause her so much turmoil when, as far as he was concerned, having her here made everything fall perfectly into place. Finally, one faction must have won, because her expression changed again. But it was to something he couldn't quite identify. Resignation, maybe. Or acceptance. Of what, though, he had no idea.

"Actually," she said, "ten thirty is pretty late, even on a Saturday, for women like me. I've been turning in a lot earlier than I used to."

Okay. He'd been turning in a little earlier himself since coming home from Wisconsin. Mostly because there hadn't been that much reason to stay up. Except for insomnia. But a couple of bourbons usually fixed that. Then her wording finally struck him.

"Women like you," he repeated. "I don't know what that means. There are no other women like you."

She managed a small smile for that. The alarm bells in his head quieted some. Not a lot. But some.

"I hope you still think that when I tell you why I've been going to bed so early."

"Unless you've been doing that so you can be with someone else, I don't think it's going to make any difference in the way I feel about you."

She bit her lip in a way he remembered her doing in Wisconsin. Mostly when she was fretting over something. "Funny you should say that," she said.

His stomach dropped. No, it wasn't. It wasn't funny at all. Not if she really was going to bed with someone else.

"I have sort of been with someone else at night. Every night."

She'd been smiling when she made the comment, but something in Tate's expression must have told her just how badly he was taking the news. Because she quickly added, "Not like that! I haven't been with anyone since... I mean, there's no one who could ever... You're the only guy who ever..."

When she realized she wasn't finishing any of her thoughts—not that they needed finishing, since Tate was getting the gist of it, and the gist of it was making him feel better, if not less confused—she expelled a restless sound, took a deep breath, then released it slowly.

Finally, she said, "I've been going to bed with someone else every night because...because I'm..."

She sighed heavily, and in a rush of words, she finished, "Because I'm pregnant, Tate."

Even though she uttered the comment in a hurry, it took a minute for him to hear it. And even though he heard it, he wasn't sure he heard it correctly. Maybe he'd misinterpreted. Did Renata just say she was—

"You're what?" he asked, just to be certain.

"I'm going to have a baby, Tate. Our baby. Yours and mine."

There wasn't any way to misinterpret that. Renata did indeed say she was pregnant. She was going to have a baby. Their baby. His and hers. Okay then. He waited for his reaction. Surely, it would be one of dread and panic. Any minute now, he would be overcome with both. Dread and panic descending in three, two, one...

But it wasn't dread or panic that overcame him. Instead, what he felt most was wonder.

He was going to have a baby? Well, not him, obviously, but half of it would be his. Would be him. Which was kind of unexpected. And kind of weird. And kind of... Wow. Kind of awesome. But it was also nowhere in his life plan. He'd never considered the prospect of becoming a father. He didn't even want the responsibility that came with having a pet. How was he supposed to accommodate a child in his life? Then again, no one said he had to. He could just mail a monthly check to Renata and skip the poopy diapers and prepubescent angst and cross-country college exploratory visits. Not to mention the birthday parties and soccer games and piano lessons that ate into a successful venture capitalist's time. A lot of men just mailed checks.

Men who were complete pricks.

"A baby?" he asked.

It was a stupid question, already answered, but he honestly didn't know what else to say. The news was still winding through his brain—and, okay, his heart. But both seemed to be greeting the new development pretty welcomingly.

When Tate said nothing in response to her clarification, Renata continued, "I know that first time we... I mean... I know that first time, I told you the timing wasn't right—and it wasn't," she hastened to add. "Not that time, anyway. But after five days of...you know... And after reading that a man's, ah, swimmers can, well, swim for anywhere from three to five days after, um, jumping into the pool, something I never really thought about but clearly should have, I guess the timing kind of got right."

When he still didn't reply—because he was still processing—she roused a cheerfulness that was clearly feigned and said, "I guess I should give you some time to think about this. I'm staying at the Knickerbocker. Room 315. Call me tomorrow, and we can meet somewhere to talk some more."

She tried to pull out of the circle of his arms, but Tate pulled her close again. "Why would you want to stay at a hotel when you can stay here with me?"

She said nothing in response to that, as if she were the one having trouble processing now.

"I mean, yeah, the Knickerbocker is great," he continued, "but it's not like home."

Not that his home had felt like home, either, for the past month. Tonight, though, it was starting to feel closer to home than it ever had before.

Renata still looked conflicted. Which was fine. Tate still felt conflicted. About some things. But none of it was about her.

She opened her mouth, hesitated, then finally said, "I just thought you might want—"

"You," he finished for her. "Renata, all I want is you. In a way, I think you're all I've ever wanted. I just didn't know it until I met you."

"But the baby will—"

"Look, I won't lie. I don't know what the baby will or won't do. And you're right. I'm going to need some time to process it. One thing I don't need to process, though, is—" He pulled her closer, kissed her again, then let her go. "You being here. With me. Nothing has been clearer in my life than how much better things are when you're around."

"But—"

He let go of her, only to place an index finger

gently against her lips to halt any further objections she might make. "But nothing," he said. "The days you and I spent together in Wisconsin were the best days of my life." He grinned. "At least until this one."

It occurred to him then that he didn't know how *she* felt about the pregnancy. She'd had more time for the realization to settle in than he had, but had it settled well? Or had it settled badly? And how did she feel about *him*? He hadn't exactly been kind to her that last day in Wisconsin. Sure, she'd traveled halfway across the country to see him tonight, but that was because the news she had to tell him wasn't the kind of thing you wanted to tell someone in a text. If she hadn't gotten pregnant, would she still be standing here right now?

"I mean, you can stay here at the house if you want to," he started to backpedal. "If you'd rather stay at the hotel…"

He actually held his breath as he waited to see how she would respond. For a moment, she didn't. Then she smiled. "I'd like that," she said. "If it isn't an imposition."

Yeah, right. What was an imposition was a hundred of his closest friends invading his house and yard, not to mention three full bars and a DJ who still had two sets to go.

"You know what?" he said impulsively. "I actually think a night at the Knickerbocker would be better."

Before she had a chance to misconstrue, he added, "Just give me ten minutes to pack a bag."

She still looked like she was going to misconstrue. Then she smiled again. Damn, he loved her smile.

"But what about your party?"

"Madison is here. So is the event planner. They can manage without me. Hell, I've spent most of the night in my room, anyway."

"Then why are you having a huge party?"

"I'll explain at the hotel. No, on the way to the hotel," he said. "Once we're at the hotel, I have something else in mind."

Her smile shone brighter. "Thank goodness I packed something other than golf-cart pajamas."

It was raining in Wisconsin. Again. But as Renny gazed through the window of her and Tate's stucco cheese wedge, she smiled. The rain this time was different, a light winter drizzle the forecasters had promised would turn to snow after dark—scarcely an hour away. Which was perfect, as tomorrow was Christmas Eve. The cottage hadn't changed much since summer, save for a good cleaning and *much* better food in the kitchen cabinets and fridge, along with a fire in the fireplace that now crackled merrily against the freezing temperatures outside.

Oh, and also the ownership. She and Tate were now co-owners of the Big Cheese Motor Inn and were planning to begin renovation on it in the spring—mid-May probably, to give them both a couple of months to cope with the addition of a baby in their lives, however that addition ended up being organized. They had plans to reopen it in a couple of summers as a family-friendly vacation destination, a throwback to another, simpler time, complete with fishing, hiking, stargazing and cave exploring...and absolutely no technology to speak of.

They had been inseparable since that night at Tate's house in July. He had returned to New York with Renny long enough for her to give her two weeks' notice at Tarrant, Fiver & Twigg and to meet her parents so they could announce together the elder Twiggs' impending grandparenthood. Her mother and father had handled the news the same way Renny and Tate had, first with surprise, then with confusion, then with delight. Since then, delight had pretty much been Renny's constant companion. She'd come back to Chicago with Tate, had rented a condo in the Gold Coast and the two had begun a courtship—for lack of a more contemporary word—that was more conducive to getting to know each other in a normal environment.

Well, except for the fact that they were already expecting a baby, something that didn't normally happen in a courtship until much later.

For Tate and Renny, though, it had worked. In

spite of her condition, they'd focused on each other first and foremost those first few months. And by the time she started to show, they were ready to start talking about and be excited by the baby. Neither of them had had a childhood they'd particularly enjoyed, and both were kind of giddy about the prospect of a do-over with their own offspring. They'd each furnished a room in their homes with a nursery. Tate was gradually cutting back on his hours at work—weekends in his home office had been the first thing to go. And Renny had launched a web-based business from home targeted at getting girls into the wilderness to discover the joys of fishing, hiking, stargazing and cave exploring. Among other things. She already had two full-time employees, and when the baby came, she'd hire a third and go down to part-time herself.

The motel would be the centerpiece for that business once it was up and running. For now, though, she and Tate were content to keep it all to themselves.

The front door opened, blowing in both the winter wind and Tate, bundled up in his spanking-new purchases from the North Face and L.L. Bean and carrying two armfuls of wood for the fire.

"Baby, it's cold outside," he said with a grin.

"Gonna get colder," she told him.

"Bring it. We're ready."

As he made his way to the fireplace to stack the

wood beside it, Renny went to the kitchen to ladle out the hot chocolate that was warming on the stove. They'd been here for a week already, long enough to hang Christmas lights, decorate a small tree and tuck a dozen presents beneath it, and they were planning to stay through New Year's. But if the weather took a turn for the worse—which she was pretty sure they were both secretly hoping would happen—they had enough supplies to last them for a month.

They couldn't stay much longer than that, though. Tate's cousin Angie the Flamethrower was getting married on Valentine's Day, and no way would they miss that. The Baccos, once Tate had decided to approach them last fall, had been nothing but warm and welcoming to him and Renny both. Apparently, Joey the Knife had been right about family being more important than anything. The Baccos couldn't wait to include Tate—and, by extension, Renny and their baby—in their lives, and Angie's wedding had seemed like the perfect place to start. As Tate's aunt Denise told him the first time they spoke, *"Chi si volta, e chi si gira, sempre a casa va finire."* Translation: "No matter where you go, you'll always end up at home." Renny figured the saying was apt in more ways than one—and for more people than the Baccos.

She returned to the living room with hot chocolate, setting Tate's mug on the coffee table and seating herself on the sofa. By now he had shed his outerwear and was down to jeans and a brown flannel shirt. His attire mirrored Renny's—especially since the striped flannel shirt she was wearing belonged to him. In one fluid move, he picked up his hot chocolate with one hand and, as had become his habit at times like this, splayed his other open over her belly.

"So, how's it been in there today?" he asked.

"Busy," she said. "Your daughter must be learning to do the mambo before she comes out."

"She's just getting ready for all the tree climbing and log rolling you have in store for her."

"Hey, you're going to learn to do those things, too, remember. This parenting thing is going to be an equal partnership. We both decided."

He started to say something else, but Baby Girl Hawthorne-Twigg—yes, after groaning at the realization of what the hyphenated last name would be, they'd decided it was too irresistible to not use it—switched from the mambo to the tarantella, turning circles in Renny's womb in a way that had become familiar to them both. As always, they laughed. Then they entwined their fingers together. Then they kissed. For a really long time.

"Only one more trimester," Renny said when they pulled apart.

He shook his head. "It's gone so fast. Hard to believe we only have three more months left of..."

When he didn't finish, she finished for him. "Of whatever this has been between us. Whatever this *is* between us."

He set his mug on the table and turned to face her but left his fingers entwined with hers on her belly. "Yeah," he said, "we should probably start trying to pin that down."

Over the past five months, they'd talked a lot about the past and even more about the future. At least, the baby's future. What they hadn't talked about much was the present. About what, exactly, the two of them were doing right now. Probably for the very reason Tate had just described—neither really seemed to know what the present was. They'd made a million plans for the baby. But they hadn't made any for themselves.

"I'm okay with the status quo," she said. Even if she kind of wasn't.

"I'm okay with it, too," he replied. Even if he didn't sound like he was. In spite of that, he added, "The status quo is pretty great."

"It is. And no one says we have to go the traditional route, right?" she said. "Lots of people who live separate lives share responsibility for their kids and do just fine."

"Right," he agreed. "They do. But we're not exactly living separate lives, are we?"

"Well, no, but…"

"But…?" he prompted.

Actually, Renny couldn't find a reason to finish her objection. Probably because she didn't have any objection to the two of them *not* living separate lives. They'd just never talked about joining their lives, that was all. Unless that was what they were doing now…

"But…" she said again. Still not sure why. Maybe in case that wasn't what they were talking about. Wondering what she would do if it wasn't, because she suddenly liked the idea a lot and wanted to talk about it.

"So, then," Tate interjected, "maybe we should talk about that aspect of whatever this—" he gestured quickly between the two of them "—is between us."

Renny's stomach lurched at his remark, and she was pretty sure it had nothing to do with the baby. Before she could say anything else, he jumped up from the sofa, went to the Christmas tree and from beneath it withdrew a small box she was positive hadn't been there before tonight. He returned to the sofa and held it up in his open palm.

"When you were a kid," he said, "did you have that tradition where you got to open one present on Christmas Eve?"

She shook her head. "My parents never let us. Even though every other kid in the neighborhood got to do it."

"Me, neither. So I think we're both entitled to open a present the night before Christmas Eve to make up for lost time."

"Then I need to get one for you to open," she said. She started to get up—and with her growing girth, she couldn't move nearly as quickly as he did—but he placed a hand gently on her shoulder and stayed her.

"In a minute," he said. "You first. Open this one."

She would have been an idiot to not entertain the possibility that it might be a ring. The box was perfectly shaped for it. It was Christmastime. They'd been inseparable for months. They were expecting a baby. But they kept separate residences. They each had a room for the baby in those residences. They hadn't once talked about taking their relationship to another level. It could just as easily be a Groupon for mommy-and-daddy-and-baby music classes or something.

She looked at the gift. Then she looked at Tate. He was smiling in a way that was at once hopeful and anxious. Probably, it wasn't a Groupon. Meaning probably, it was a…

Carefully, she accepted the present from him. It was wrapped in forest green foil and had a bow as silver as a crystal lake. As she gingerly unwrapped it, the baby began to move inside her again, probably in response to her quickening pulse and the way the blood was rushing through her body. The crackle of the fire and patter of the rain dulled to faint whispers, and the air in the room seemed to come alive. Tate watched her intently until she had her fingers poised to open the box beneath the paper, but he didn't say a word. So Renny slowly pushed the top upward.

Not a Groupon. Definitely a ring. In fact, it was the most beautiful ring she'd ever seen.

"The stone is from one of the interesting rocks we found that day on our hike," he told her. "The quartz one. It was the same color as the blackberries we picked. And I had the jeweler set it in silver because the stars that last night were like silver. And the pattern around the band is like the pinecones we found. I hope you don't think it's too corny."

He sounded as excited as…well, a kid on Christmas as he told her the reasons he'd had the ring fashioned the way he had. As if she'd needed him to explain any of that. The moment Renny saw it, all those things flooded into her head—and then her heart. And now, every time she looked at the ring on her finger, she would remember and feel them again.

"It's not corny," she said softly. "It's beautiful."

He expelled a relieved sound. "Then it's yes?"

Whatever he was asking, her answer was yes.

Just to be sure he was asking the same question she wanted him to be asking, though, she replied, "Is what yes?"

He looked confused for a moment, then thoughtful. "I never said it out loud, did I? I thought it like ten times while you were unwrapping the ring, but I never actually asked the question, did I?"

Not to be coy, but... "What question?" she asked.

"The one about us...you and me...getting married."

Oh, *that* question. "Depends," she said.

He looked slightly less relieved, slightly less hopeful, slightly more anxious. "On what?"

"On why you're asking. Is it because of the baby?"

He shook his head. "No. It's because of you. Because the last five months have been the best time of my life, rivaled only by five days in June that I never thought could be topped." He took the box from her hand and plucked the ring from its nest. "I love you, Renata Twigg. I think I fell in love with you the minute I saw you standing in the rain outside a giant wedge of cheese." He smiled again, and this time there was only contentment in his expression. "And I will love you until we're both food for the fishies."

Oh. Well. In that case...

"Will you marry me?" he finally asked.

"Of course I'll marry you," she was finally able to say. "I mean, I have to, don't I?"

His contentment slipped a bit. "Why? Because of the baby?"

She shook her head. "No. Because I love you, Tate Hawthorne. I think I fell in love with you the minute I saw you in those zip-up leather polo boots. That I immediately wanted to *unzip*. With my teeth."

He looked mildly shocked, then not-so-mildly turned on. "Unfortunately, I left them at home. But you know…" He arched an eyebrow suggestively. "These hiking boots aren't going to remove themselves. And neither are any of these other things."

Renny arched an eyebrow right back. "Well, in that case, what are we waiting for?"

"Nothing," he said. "We have all the time in the world."

Indeed, they did. Even better, it was a world that exceeded their wildest dreams. A world they had created together. A world where they both belonged.

* * * * *

If you like sexy and steamy stories with strong heroines and irresistible heroes, you'll love FORGED IN DESIRE by New York Times *bestselling author Brenda Jackson—featuring Margo Connelly and Lamar "Striker" Jennings, the reformed bad boy who'll do anything to protect her, even if it means lowering the defenses around his own heart...*

Turn the page for a sneak peek at FORGED IN DESIRE!

PROLOGUE

"FINALLY, WE GET to go home."

Margo Connelly was certain the man's words echoed the sentiment they all felt. The last thing she'd expected when reporting for jury duty was to be sequestered during the entire trial...especially with twelve strangers, more than a few of whom had taken the art of bitching to a whole new level.

She was convinced this had been the longest, if not the most miserable, six weeks of her life, as well as a lousy way to start off the new year. They hadn't been allowed to have any inbound or outbound calls, read the newspapers, check any emails, watch television or listen to the radio. The only good thing was, with the vote just taken, a unanimous decision had been reached and justice would be served. The federal case against Murphy Erickson would finally be over and they would be allowed to go home.

"It's time to let the bailiff know we've reached a decision," Nancy Snyder spoke up, interrupting Margo's thoughts. "I have a man waiting at home, who I haven't seen in six weeks, and I can't wait to get to him."

Lucky you, Margo thought, leaning back in her chair. She and Scott Dylan had split over a year ago, and the parting hadn't been pretty.

Fortunately, as a wedding-dress designer, she could work from anywhere and had decided to move back home to Charlottesville. She could be near her uncle Frazier, her father's brother and the man who'd become her guardian when her parents had died in a house fire when she was ten. He was her only living relative and, although they often butted heads, she had missed him while living in New York.

A knock on the door got everyone's attention. The bailiff had arrived. Hopefully, in a few hours it would all be over and the judge would release them. She couldn't wait to get back to running her business. Six weeks had been a long time away. Lucky for her she had finished her last order in time for the bride's Christmas wedding. But she couldn't help wondering how many new orders she might have missed while on jury duty.

The bailiff entered and said, "The judge has called the court back in session for the reading of the verdict. We're ready to escort you there."

Like everyone else in the room, Margo stood. She was ready for the verdict to be read. It was only after this that she could get her life back.

"FOREMAN, HAS THE JURY reached a verdict?" the judge asked.

"Yes, we have, Your Honor."

The courtroom was quiet as the verdict was read. "We, the jury, find Murphy Erickson guilty of murder."

Suddenly Erickson bowled over and laughed. It made the hairs on the necks of everyone in attendance stand up. The outburst prompted the judge to hit his gavel several times. "Order in the courtroom. Counselor, quiet the defendant or he will be found in contempt of court."

"I don't give a damn about any contempt," Erickson snarled loudly. "You!" he said, pointing a finger at the judge. "Along with everyone else in this courtroom, you have just signed your own death warrant. As long as I remain locked up, someone in here will die every seventy-two hours." His gaze didn't miss a single individual.

Pandemonium broke out. The judge pounded his gavel, trying to restore order. Police officers rushed forward to subdue Erickson and haul him away. But the sound of his threats echoed loudly in Margo's ears.

CHAPTER ONE

Lamar "Striker" Jennings walked into the hospital room, stopped and then frowned. "What the hell is he doing working from bed?"

"I asked myself the same thing when I got his call for us to come here," Striker's friend Quasar Patterson said, sitting lazily in a chair with his long legs stretched out in front of him.

"And you might as well take a seat like he told us to do," another friend, Stonewall Courson, suggested, while pointing to an empty chair. "Evidently it will take more than a bullet to slow down Roland."

Roland Summers, CEO of Summers Security Firm, lay in the hospital bed, staring at them. Had it been just last week that the man had been fighting for his life after foiling an attempted carjacking?

"You still look like shit, Roland. Shouldn't you be trying to get some rest instead of calling a meeting?" Striker asked, sliding his tall frame into the chair. He didn't like seeing Roland this way. They'd been friends a long time, and he couldn't ever recall the man being sick. Not even with a cold. Well, at least he was alive. That damn bullet could have taken him out and Striker didn't want to think about that.

"You guys have been keeping up with the news?" Roland asked in a strained voice, interrupting Striker's thoughts.

"We're aware of what's going on, if that's what you want to know," Stonewall answered. "Nobody took Murphy Erickson's threat seriously."

Roland made an attempt to nod his head. "And now?"

"And now people are panicking. Phones at the office have been ringing off the hook. I'm sure every protective security service in town is booked solid. Everyone in the courtroom that day is either in hiding or seeking protection, and with good reason," Quasar piped in to say. "The judge, clerk reporter and bailiff are all dead. All three were gunned down within seventy-two hours of each other."

"The FBI is working closely with local law enforcement, and they figure it's the work of the same assassin," Striker added. "I heard they anticipate he'll go after someone on the jury next."

"Which is why I called the three of you here. There was a woman on the jury who I want protected. It's personal."

"Personal?" Striker asked, lifting a brow. He knew Roland dated off and on, but he'd never been serious with anyone. He was always quick to say that his wife, Becca, had been his one and only love.

"Yes, personal. She's a family member."

The room got quiet. That statement was even more baffling since, as far as the three of them knew, Roland didn't have any family...at least not anymore. They were all aware of his history. He'd been a cop, who'd discovered some of his fellow officers on the take. Before he could blow the whistle he'd been framed and sent to prison for fifteen years. Becca had refused to accept his fate and worked hard to get him a new trial. He served three years before finally leaving prison but not before the dirty cops murdered Roland's wife. All the cops involved had eventually been brought to justice and charged with the death of Becca Summers, in addition to other crimes.

"You said she's family?" Striker asked, looking confused.

"Yes, although I say that loosely since we've never officially met. I know who she is, but she doesn't know I even exist." Roland then closed his eyes, and Striker knew he had to be in pain.

"Man, you need to rest," Quasar spoke up. "You can cover this with us another time."

Roland's eyes flashed back open. "No, we need to talk now. I need one of you protecting her right away."

Nobody said anything for a minute and then Striker asked, "What relation is she to you, man?"

"My niece. To make a long story short, years ago my mom got involved with a married man. He broke things off when his wife found out about the affair but not before I was conceived. I always knew the identity of my father. I also knew about his other two, older sons, although they didn't know about me. I guess you can say I was the old man's secret.

"One day after I'd left for college, I got a call from my mother letting me know the old man was dead but he'd left me something in his will."

Striker didn't say anything, thinking that at least Roland's old man had done right by him in the end. To this day, his own poor excuse of a father hadn't even acknowledged his existence. "That's when your two brothers found out about you?" he asked.

"Yes. Their mother found out about me, as well. She turned out to be a real bitch. Even tried blocking what Connelly had left for me in the will. But she couldn't. The old man evidently had anticipated her making such a move and made sure the will was ironclad. He gave me enough to finish college without taking out student loans with a little left over."

"Good for him," Quasar said. "What about your brothers? How did they react to finding out about you?"

"The eldest acted like a dickhead," Roland said without pause. "The other one's reaction was just the opposite. His name was Murdock and he reached out to me afterward. I would hear from him from time to time. He would call to see how I was doing."

Roland didn't say anything for a minute, his face showing he was struggling with strong emotions. "Murdock is the one who gave Becca the money to hire a private investigator to reopen my case. I never got the chance to thank him."

"Why?" Quasar asked.

Roland drew in a deep breath and then said, "Murdock and his wife were killed weeks before my new trial began."

"How did they die?"

"House fire. Fire department claimed faulty wiring. I never believed it but couldn't prove otherwise. Luckily their ten-year-old daughter wasn't home at the time. She'd been attending a sleepover at one of her friends' houses."

"You think those dirty cops took them out, too?" Stonewall asked.

"Yes. While I could link Becca's death to those corrupt cops, there wasn't enough evidence to connect Murdock's and his wife's deaths."

Stonewall nodded. "What happened to the little girl after that?"

"She was raised by the other brother. Since the old lady had died by then, he became her guardian." Roland paused a minute and then added, "He came to see me this morning."

"Who? Your brother? The dickhead?" Quasar asked with a snort.

"Yes," Roland said, and it was obvious he was trying not to grin. "When he walked in here it shocked the hell out of me. Unlike Murdock, he never reached out to me, and I think he even resented Murdock for doing so."

"So what the fuck was his reason for showing up here today?" Stonewall asked. "He'd heard you'd gotten shot and wanted to show some brotherly concern?" It was apparent by Stonewall's tone he didn't believe that was the case.

"Umm, let me guess," Quasar then said languidly. "He had a change of heart, especially now that his niece's life is in danger. Now he wants your help. I assume this is the same niece you want protected."

"Yes, to both. He'd heard I'd gotten shot and claimed he was concerned. Although he's not as much of a dickhead as before, I sensed a little resentment is still there. But not because I'm his father's bastard—a part of me believes he's gotten over that."

"What, then?" Striker asked.

"I think he blames me for Murdock's death. He didn't come out and say that, but he did let me know he was aware of the money Murdock gave Becca to get me a new trial and that he has similar suspicions regarding the cause of their deaths. That's why, when he became his niece's guardian, he sent her out of the country to attend an all-girls school with tight security in London for a few years. He didn't bring her back to the States until after those bad cops were sent to jail."

"So the reason he showed up today was because he thought sending you on a guilt trip would be the only way to get you to protect your niece?" Striker asked angrily. Although Roland had tried hiding it, Striker could clearly see the pain etched in his face whenever he spoke.

"Evidently. I guess it didn't occur to him that making sure she is protected is something I'd want to do. I owe Murdock, although I don't owe Frazier Connelly a damn thing."

"Frazier Connelly?" Quasar said, sitting up straight in his chair. "*The* Frazier Connelly of Connelly Enterprises?"

"One and the same."

Nobody said anything for a while. Then Striker asked, "Your niece—what's her name?"

"Margo. Margo Connelly."

"And she doesn't know anything about you?" Stonewall asked. "Are you still the family's well-kept secret?"

Roland nodded. "Frazier confirmed that today, and I prefer things to stay that way. If I could, I would protect her. I can't, so I need one of you to do it for me. Hopefully, it won't be long before the assassin that Erickson hired is apprehended."

Striker eased out of his chair. Roland, of all people, knew that, in addition to working together, he, Quasar and Stonewall were the best of friends. They looked out for each other and watched each other's back. And if needed they would cover Roland's back, as well. Roland was more than just their employer—he was their close friend, mentor and the voice of reason, even when they really didn't want one. "Stonewall is handling things at the office in your absence, and Quasar is already working a case. That leaves me. Don't worry about a thing, Roland. I've got it covered. Consider it done."

MARGO CONNELLY STARED up at her uncle. "A bodyguard? Do you really think that's necessary, Uncle Frazier? I understand extra policemen are patrolling the streets."

"That's not good enough. Why should I trust a bunch of police officers?"

"Why shouldn't you?" she countered, not for the first time wondering what her uncle had against cops.

"I have my reasons, but this isn't about me—this is about you and your safety. I refuse to have you placed in any danger. What's the big deal? You've had a bodyguard before."

Yes, she'd had one before. Right after her parents'

deaths, when her uncle had become her guardian. He had shipped her off to London for three years. She'd reckoned he'd been trying to figure out what he, a devout bachelor, was to do with a ten-year-old. When she returned to the United States, Apollo remained her bodyguard. When she turned fourteen, she fought hard for a little personal freedom. But she'd always known the chauffeurs Uncle Frazier hired could do more than drive her to and from school. More than once she'd seen the guns they carried.

"Yes, but that was then and this is now, Uncle Frazier. I can look after myself."

"Haven't you been keeping up with the news?" he snapped. "Three people are dead. All three were in that courtroom with you. Erickson is making sure his threat is carried out."

"And more than likely whoever is committing these murders will be caught before there can be another shooting. I understand the three were killed while they were away from home. I have enough paperwork to catch up on here for a while. I didn't even leave my house today."

"You don't think a paid assassin will find you here? Alone? You either get on board with having a bodyguard or you move back home. It's well secured there."

Margo drew in a deep breath. Back home was the Connelly estate. Yes, it was secure, with its state-of-the-art surveillance system. While growing up, she'd thought of the ten-acre property, surrounded by a tall wrought iron fence and cameras watching her every move, as a prison. Now she couldn't stand the thought of staying there for any long period of time...especially if Liz was still in residence.

Margo's forty-five-year-old uncle had never married and claimed he had his reasons for never wanting to. But that didn't keep him from occasionally having a live-in mistress under his roof. His most recent was Liz Tillman and, as far as Margo was concerned, the woman was a *gold digger*.

"It's final. A bodyguard will be here around the clock to protect you until this madness is over."

Margo didn't say anything. She wondered if at any time it had crossed her uncle's mind that they were at her house, not his, and she was no longer a child but a twenty-six-year-old woman. In a way she knew she should appreciate his concern, but she refused to let anyone order her around.

He was wrong in assuming she hadn't been keeping up with the news. Just because she was trying to maintain a level head didn't mean a part of her wasn't a little worried.

She frowned as she glanced up at him. The last thing she wanted was for him to worry needlessly about her. "I'll give this bodyguard a try...but he better be forewarned not to get underfoot. I have a lot of work to do." She wasn't finished yet. "And another thing, Uncle Frazier," she said, crossing her arms over her chest. "I think you forget sometimes that I'm twenty-six and live on my own. Just because I'm going along with you on this, I hope you don't think you can start bulldozing your way with me."

He glowered at her. "You're stubborn like your father."

She smiled. "I'll take that as a compliment." Dropping her hands, she moved back toward the sofa and sat down, grabbing a magazine off the coffee table to flip through. "So, when do we hire this bodyguard?"

"He's been hired. In fact, I expect him to arrive in a few minutes."

Margo's head jerked up. "What?"

Find out what happens when Margo and Striker come face-to-face in FORGED IN DESIRE by New York Times *bestselling author Brenda Jackson.*

Available February 2017 from Brenda Jackson and HQN Books.

COMING NEXT MONTH FROM

HARLEQUIN *Desire*

Available April 4, 2017

#2509 THE TEN-DAY BABY TAKEOVER
Billionaires and Babies • by Karen Booth
When Sarah Daltry barges into billionaire Aiden Langford's office with his secret baby, he strikes a deal—help him out for ten days as the nanny and he'll help with her new business. Love isn't part of the deal...

#2510 EXPECTING THE BILLIONAIRE'S BABY
Texas Cattleman's Club: Blackmail • by Andrea Laurence
Thirteen years after their breakup, Deacon Chase and Cecelia Morgan meet again...and now he's her billionaire boss! But while Deacon unravels the secrets between them, Cecelia discovers she has a little surprise in store for him, as well...

#2511 PRIDE AND PREGNANCY
by Sarah M. Anderson
Secretly wealthy FBI agent Tom Yellow Bird always puts the job first. But whisking sexy Caroline away to his luxury cabin is above and beyond. And when they end up in bed—and expecting!—it could compromise the most important case of his career...

#2512 HIS EX'S WELL-KEPT SECRET
The Ballantyne Brothers • by Joss Wood
Their weekend in Milan led to a child, but after an accident, rich jeweler Jaeger Ballantyne can't remember any of it! Now Piper Mills is back in his life, asking for his help, and once again he can't resist her...

#2513 THE MAGNATE'S MAIL-ORDER BRIDE
The McNeill Magnates • by Joanne Rock
When a Manhattan billionaire sets his sights on ballerina Sofia Koslov for a marriage of convenience to cover up an expensive family scandal, will she gain the freedom she's always craved, or will it cost her everything?

#2514 A BEAUTY FOR THE BILLIONAIRE
Accidental Heirs • by Elizabeth Bevarly
Hogan has inherited a fortune! He's gone from mechanic to billionaire overnight and can afford to win back the socialite who once broke his heart. So he hires his ex's favorite chef, Chloe, to lure her in, but soon he's falling for the wrong woman...

This was a mistake. Jonathan Bear was absolutely certain
of it. But he had earned millions making mistakes, so
what was one more? Nobody else had responded to his
ad.

Except for this pale, strange little creature who looked
barely twenty and wore the outfit of an eighty-year-old
woman.

She was… Well, she wasn't the kind of formidable
woman who could stand up to the rigors of working with
him.

His sister, Rebecca, would say—with absolutely no
tact at all—that he sucked as a boss. And maybe she was
right, but he didn't really care. He was busy, and right
now he hated most of what he was busy with.

There was irony in that, he knew. He had worked
hard all his life. He had built everything he had, brick by

brick. And every brick built a stronger wall against all the things he had left behind. Poverty, uncertainty, the lack of respect.

Finally, Jonathan Bear, that poor Indian kid who wasn't worth anything to anyone, bastard son of the biggest bastard in town, had his house on the side of the mountain and more money than he would ever be able to spend.

And he was bored out of his mind.

Boredom, it turned out, worked him into a hell of a temper. He had a feeling Hayley Thompson wasn't strong enough to stand up to that. But he expected to go through a few assistants before he found one who could handle it. She might as well be number one.

"You've got the job," he said. "You can start tomorrow."

Her eyes widened, and he noticed they were a strange shade of blue. Gray in some lights, shot through with a dark, velvet navy that reminded him of the ocean before a storm. It made him wonder if there was some hidden strength there.

They would both find out.

Don't miss
SEDUCE ME, COWBOY
by New York Times *bestselling author Maisey Yates,
available November 2016 wherever
Harlequin® Desire books and ebooks are sold.*

www.Harlequin.com

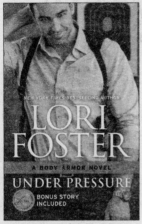